Taken By The Mob Boss

A Dark Mafia Romance Series, Volume 1

Lexy Timms

Published by Dark Shadow Publishing, 2021.

This is a work of fiction. Similarities to real people, places, or events are entirely coincidental.

TAKEN BY THE MOB BOSS

First edition. March 16, 2021.

Copyright © 2021 Lexy Timms.

Written by Lexy Timms.

Also by Lexy Timms

A Bad Boy Bullied Romance
I Hate You
I Hate You A Little Bit
I Hate You A Little Bit More

A Burning Love Series
Spark of Passion
Flame of Desire
Blaze of Ecstasy

A Chance at Forever Series
Forever Perfect
Forever Desired
Forever Together

A Dark Mafia Romance Series
Taken By The Mob Boss

A Dating App Series
I've Been Matched
You've Been Matched
We've Been Matched

A "Kind of" Billionaire
Taking a Risk
Safety in Numbers
Pretend You're Mine

A Maybe Series
Maybe I Should
Maybe I Shouldn't
Maybe I Did

Assisting the Boss Series
Billion Reasons
Duke of Delegation
Late Night Meetings
Delegating Love
Suitors and Admirers

BBW Romance Series
Capturing Her Beauty

Pursuing Her Dreams
Tracing Her Curves

Beating the Biker Series
Making Her His
Making the Break
Making of Them

Betrayal at the Bay Series
Devil's Bay
Devil's Deceit

Billionaire Banker Series
Banking on Him
Price of Passion
Investing in Love
Knowing Your Worth
Treasured Forever
Banking on Christmas
Billionaire Banker Box Set Books #1-3

Billionaire CEO Brothers
Tempting the Player
Late Night Boardroom
Reviewing the Perfomance
Result of Passion

Directing the Next Move
Touching the Assets

Billionaire Holiday Romance Series
Driving Home for Christmas
The Valentine Getaway
Cruising Love
Billionaire Holiday Romance Box Set

Billionaire in Disguise Series
Facade
Illusion
Charade

Billionaire Secrets Series
The Secret
Freedom
Courage
Trust
Impulse
Billionaire Secrets Box Set Books #1-3

Blind Sight Series
See Me
Fix Me
Eyes On Me

Forbidding Desire
Craving Passion

Dominating PA Series
Her Personal Assistant - Part 1
Her Personal Assistant - Part 2
Her Personal Assistant Box Set

Fake Billionaire Series
Faking It
Temporary CEO
Caught in the Act
Never Tell A Lie
Fake Christmas
Fake Billionaire Box Set #1-3

Firehouse Romance Series
Caught in Flames
Burning With Desire
Craving the Heat
Firehouse Romance Complete Collection

Forging Billions Series
Dirty Money
Petty Cash
Payment Required

For His Pleasure
Elizabeth
Georgia
Madison

Fortune Riders MC Series
Billionaire Biker
Billionaire Ransom
Billionaire Misery
Fortune Riders Box Set - Books #1-3

Fragile Series
Fragile Touch
Fragile Kiss
Fragile Love

Great Temptation Series
The Devil's Footsteps
Heaven's Command
Mortals Surrender

Hades' Spawn Motorcycle Club
One You Can't Forget
One That Got Away

Your Move
Green With Envy
Saving Money

Highlander Wolf Series
Pack Run
Pack Land
Pack Rules

Hollyweird Fae Series
Inception of Gold
Disruption of Magic
Guardians of Twilight

How To Love A Spy
The Secret
The Secret Life
The Secret Wife

Just About Series
About Love
About Truth
About Forever
Just About Box Set Books #1-3

Justice Series
Seeking Justice
Finding Justice
Chasing Justice
Pursuing Justice
Justice - Complete Series

Karma Series
Walk Away
Make Him Pay

Kissed by Billions
Kissed by Passion
Kissed by Desire
Kissed by Love

Leaning Towards Trouble
Trouble
Discord
Tenacity

Love on the Sea Series
Ships Ahoy
Rough Sea

High Tide

Love You Series
Love Life
Need Love
My Love

Managing the Billionaire
Never Enough
Worth the Cost
Secret Admirers
Chasing Affection
Pressing Romance
Timeless Memories
Managing the Billionaire Box Set Books #1-3

Managing the Bosses Series
The Boss
The Boss Too
Who's the Boss Now
Love the Boss
I Do the Boss
Wife to the Boss
Employed by the Boss
Brother to the Boss
Senior Advisor to the Boss
Forever the Boss
Christmas With the Boss

Billionaire in Control
Billionaire Makes Millions
Billionaire at Work
Precious Little Thing
Priceless Love
Valentine Love
The Cost of Freedom
Trick or Treat
The Night Before Christmas
Gift for the Boss - Novella 3.5
Managing the Bosses Box Set #1-3
Managing the Bosses Novellas

Mislead by the Bad Boy Series
Deceived
Provoked
Betrayed

Model Mayhem Series
Shameless
Modesty
Imperfection

Moment in Time
Highlander's Bride
Victorian Bride
Modern Day Bride
A Royal Bride

Forever the Bride

Mountain Millionaire Series
Close to the Ridge
Crossing the Bluff
Climbing the Mount

My Best Friend's Sister
Hometown Calling
A Perfect Moment
Thrown in Together

My Darker Side Series
Darkest Hour
Time to Stop
Against the Light

Neverending Dream Series
Neverending Dream - Part 1
Neverending Dream - Part 2
Neverending Dream - Part 3
Neverending Dream - Part 4
Neverending Dream - Part 5

Outside the Octagon

Submit
Fight
Knockout

Protecting Diana Series
Her Bodyguard
Her Defender
Her Champion
Her Protector
Her Forever
Protecting Diana Box Set Books #1-3

Protecting Layla Series
His Mission
His Objective
His Devotion

Racing Hearts Series
Rush
Pace
Fast

Regency Romance Series
The Duchess Scandal - Part 1
The Duchess Scandal - Part 2

Reverse Harem Series
Primals
Archaic
Unitary

RIP Series
Track the Ripper
Hunt the Ripper
Pursue the Ripper

R&S Rich and Single Series
Alex Reid
Parker
Sebastian

Saving Forever
Saving Forever - Part 1
Saving Forever - Part 2
Saving Forever - Part 3
Saving Forever - Part 4
Saving Forever - Part 5
Saving Forever - Part 6
Saving Forever Part 7
Saving Forever - Part 8
Saving Forever Boxset Books #1-3

Secrets & Lies Series
Strange Secrets
Evading Secrets
Inspiring Secrets
Lies and Secrets
Mastering Secrets
Alluring Secrets
Secrets & Lies Box Set Books #1-3

Shifting Desires Series
Jungle Heat
Jungle Fever
Jungle Blaze

Sin Series
Payment for Sin
Atonement Within
Declaration of Love

Southern Romance Series
Little Love Affair
Siege of the Heart
Freedom Forever
Soldier's Fortune

Spanked Series
Passion
Playmate
Pleasure

Spelling Love Series
The Author
The Book Boyfriend
The Words of Love

Taboo Wedding Series
He Loves Me Not
With This Ring
Happily Ever After

Tattooist Series
Confession of a Tattooist
Surrender of a Tattooist
Heart of a Tattooist
Hopes & Dreams of a Tattooist

Tennessee Romance
Whisky Lullaby
Whisky Melody

Whisky Harmony

The Bad Boy Alpha Club
Battle Lines - Part 1
Battle Lines

The Brush Of Love Series
Every Night
Every Day
Every Time
Every Way
Every Touch
The Brush of Love Series Box Set Books #1-3

The Debt
The Debt: Part 1 - Damn Horse
The Debt: Complete Collection

The Fire Inside Series
Dare Me
Defy Me
Burn Me

The Gentleman's Club Series
Gambler

Player
Wager

The Golden Mail
Hot Off the Press
Extra! Extra!
Read All About It
Stop the Press
Breaking News
This Just In
The Golden Mail Box Set Books #1-3

The Lucky Billionaire Series
Lucky Break
Streak of Luck
Lucky in Love

The Sound of Breaking Hearts Series
Disruption
Destroy
Devoted

The University of Gatica Series
The Recruiting Trip
Faster
Higher

Stronger
Dominate
No Rush
University of Gatica - The Complete Series

T.N.T. Series
Troubled Nate Thomas - Part 1
Troubled Nate Thomas - Part 2
Troubled Nate Thomas - Part 3

Toxic Touch Series
Noxious
Lethal
Willful
Tainted
Craved

Undercover Series
Perfect For Me
Perfect For You
Perfect For Us

Unknown Identity Series
Unknown
Unpublished
Unexposed

Unsure
Unwritten
Unknown Identity Box Set: Books #1-3

Unlucky Series
Unlucky in Love
UnWanted
UnLoved Forever

War Torn Letters Series
My Sweetheart
My Darling
My Beloved

Wet & Wild Series
Stormy Love
Savage Love
Secure Love

Worth It Series
Worth Billions
Worth Every Cent
Worth More Than Money

You & Me - A Bad Boy Romance

Just Me
Touch Me
Kiss Me

Standalone
Wash
Loving Charity
Summer Lovin'
Love & College
Billionaire Heart
First Love
Frisky and Fun Romance Box Collection
Beating Hades' Bikers
Everyone Loves a Bad Boy

Watch for more at www.lexytimms.com.

TAKEN BY THE MOB BOSS

A DARK MAFIA ROMANCE BOOK ONE

USA TODAY BESTSELLING AUTHOR

LEXY TIMMS

Copyright 2021 By LEXY TIMMS

A Dark Mafia Romance Series

Book 1 – Taken By The Mob Boss
Book 2 – Truce With The Mob Boss
Book 3 – Taking Over The Mob Boss
Book 4 – Trouble For The Mob Boss
Book 5 – Tailored By The Mob Boss
Book 6 – Tricking By The Mob Boss

Find Lexy Timms:

LEXY TIMMS NEWSLETTER:
http://eepurl.com/9i0vD
Lexy Timms Facebook Page:
https://www.facebook.com/SavingForever
Lexy Timms Website:
http://www.lexytimms.com

Want to read more...
For **FREE**?
Sign up for Lexy Timms' newsletter
And she'll send you updates on new releases, ARC copies of books
and a whole lotta fun!
Sign up for news and updates!
http://eepurl.com/9i0vD

Taken By The Mob Boss

EVIL begins when you start to treat people as things...

A KIDNAPPING ISN'T how I expected to meet the woman of my dreams.

But when my brother, intent on proving himself as the hardcore gangster he wants to be, comes up with the idea to kidnap the daughter of a powerful crime boss, I know I can't stop him. And that's how I meet Charlotte.

Beautiful, intelligent, graceful – and hurting from the life she's been trapped into living. She wants to get out of this world just as much as I do, and it doesn't take long till we fall for each other, hard and fast.

Except time is running out for both of us.

If we're going to be together, we need to act fast – and do something that we can never renege on...

Chapter One

Charlotte

I PUSHED MY FOOD AROUND the plate in front of me. I didn't much feel like eating.

"Are you all right, darling?" my father asked me, leaning forward with concern. I felt Matt's hand dig into my thigh under the table – not an affectionate gesture, but a warning.

"I'm fine," I told him quickly, plastering a smile on to my face. "Just...tired, that's all."

"What from?" He narrowed his eyes at me. He had every right to wonder. He knew that I didn't do a whole hell of a lot around here, and that if something had gotten under my skin, he needed to know about it.

I took a deep breath, wishing that I could come out and tell him the truth. That I was exhausted because the man who was supposed to love me had taken out his anger on me the day before – that he had decided I'd come home too late for his liking and had left a bruise the length of his finger on my jaw, and I'd had to spend a half-hour putting make-up over it before I came out to meet with my father for lunch. If I had breathed a word of it, though, I knew that the grip on my leg would only have gotten harder, and I didn't want to have to deal with the blow-back if I told him what was truly happening here.

"Just wedding planning," I replied as brightly as I could manage. "The venue that I had decided on fell through, so I had to find something else to fix that."

"You need me to get in touch with them?" my father asked, and I could hear the edge to his voice that told me that the contact would be far from friendly. I had to stifle a giggle at the thought of it – him sending his thugs down to some bougie wedding planner to try and talk some sense into her. Yeah, I was sure that would go down a storm.

"No, I don't, Daddy," I assured him. "The wedding is still nine months away. We have plenty of time to get everything in order."

"Right," Matt replied, and he slid his arm along the back of my seat in a way that could have been mistaken for affectionate if you didn't know better. I tried not to tense my shoulders and pull away from him on instinct. I had to convince everyone here that this was the very picture of a functioning relationship. Because if I didn't...

If I didn't, he would make me pay. And I didn't want to deal with that. Not now. Not again.

That was the problem with Matt. He thought that the best thing he could do was convince everyone around him that he was in charge, convince them that he was a good partner to me and that my father had made the right choice in taking him into the family. He had already worked for my father for years by the time we got engaged – notice that I don't describe it as a proposal, because it wasn't. He went from being just some idiot that I avoided around the house at all costs to being my husband-to-be with no warning at all, and I was still resentful as hell that I'd had to go through all of that. Mad that my father had truly believed that I could be happy with a man as foul as him.

He could have just worked on his temper, put in some effort to not be as big of a shithead as he normally was, but that was never how it had worked for Matt. He was set in his ways, certain that he was going to take control of the empire by the time that my father stepped back from it; he saw himself as the next Lou, a young man dedicated to the game and willing to do anything to help the family.

As long as that family wasn't me, of course.

And at this point, even if he spent the rest of his life trying to make it up to me, I doubted that I would be able to get past everything that he had done. It was just too much, far too much to live with. I would never get over the memories of what he had done to me, the way he had treated me, the way he had touched me like I was nothing more than an annoyance to his life at large. I was a means to an end to him, and that meant that I didn't deserve the respect that he would have given anyone else.

Even though I despised my engagement to this man, I couldn't blame my father for setting me up with him. After all, he had no idea what Matt had done, what he was like. He had only ever seen him as a right-hand man, someone who had an answer to every question. My father hadn't considered whether that would translate into a marriage or not.

Nine months. Less than a year. As Matt and my father talked, I found my mind drifting off, focusing on that number. So close. It was so close. And once I was married, I knew that I would be stuck with him for life. That was how it worked. He was never going to let me go, never going to let me leave him, because I was his assurance that he could never be booted from the family. My father was never going to get rid of his son-in-law, and that meant it was up to me to swallow his bad behavior and hope that I survived it.

The worst part of it was knowing that, even if I had come clean to someone about what he had done – even if I turned up to this lunch with bruises on my face, didn't drape myself in scarfs and flowy clothes to cover up the reminders of what he had done to me, people would have found a way to prove that I was the one who had caused all of this. They would look at me and wonder what I had done or what I had failed to do to make him treat me like that, or they would have just outright denied that he was capable of it in the first place. If I could have grabbed someone by the shoulders, shaken them, told them that *any* man who got involved with this line of work out of choice clearly had no problem with violence, and that he wouldn't be afraid to bring that violence home to the people he was supposed to love most...

"Charlotte?"

I looked up. My father was smiling at me. I knew that, despite it all, he did care about me – he did want me to be happy, even though sometimes it was hard for me to remember that. He didn't know that the other man sitting at this table with us would push me off my feet the moment we were back through the door to our shared space if he thought that I hadn't tried hard enough.

"Yes?" I replied, smiling quickly, shooting a furtive look at Matt and hoping that he wasn't pissed at me. He was smiling, that rictus grin, the one that at least told me that I was doing the right thing.

"Come by the house when you get the chance. We can talk some more about the wedding," he replied. I nodded. I knew that he didn't really care about the details of this wedding, but he was trying to connect with me. It would have been sweet if the thought of the wedding didn't make me want to throw up what little I'd managed to have of my salad onto the ground in front of me.

My father insisted on paying, and he dropped a kiss on my cheek before he guided me to the car. I knew that he wanted to ask me something, that he sensed something was off, but I didn't have the words to tell him what it was. I never would. I knew he would never believe me, anyway.

Matt drove us home, and I rested my head against the cool glass and peered out of the window as we drove. I didn't want to be here. I knew that much. That was about the only thing in my life that I could rely on, that certainty that I wanted to get out of here, that sureness that I wanted to leave him and this life—get out for good.

We pulled up outside the house, and I followed him back inside, my heart beating hard in my chest as I went. If I had made a single mistake, whether I knew it or not, this was where I would find out. This was where he would make it clear that he wasn't going to stand for my failures.

But instead of confronting me, cornering me back against the door, he was focused on his phone by the time I got in. He was talking to another woman, I was sure of it – I checked his phone sometimes, when he was in the shower, and he constantly had stacks of borderline-illiterate conversations going on with women who didn't even know he was engaged. It should have pissed me off, but if anything, it was a relief – I knew that he would be out of the house for a while when he was focusing on them, and at least I wouldn't have to worry about his anger turning on me.

"You did good today, baby," he told me off-handedly. I hated when he called me that. The pet names sounded like threats or jokes coming out of his mouth, and I knew that I would never be able to hear them from someone else without thinking of the twisted way he said them.

"I'll be back later tonight. Don't wait up," he continued without lifting his eyes from his phone. I hoped that whoever was on the other end of that knew what they were getting– I hoped that she was going to be able to handle him. I knew that I got the worst of him, but at least that meant that I didn't send him out into the world to do worse to other women.

"Bye," I muttered as he brushed past me again and out the door. A moment later, the house was quiet – and I couldn't help but feel a rush of relief as the door clicked shut behind him.

This was the man that I was supposed to spend the rest of my life with. The man who was going to come home to me day after day, night after night. The one I would have to handle, no matter what. As I sank down on to the edge of the couch, inhaling the silence, the quiet, I knew that I was well and truly fucked. There was no way that I could get out of this wedding now. But if I went through with it, I would be tied to that fucker for life.

But I couldn't see a way out of it. I had considered every path, every route that would have gotten me away from him, and nothing had brought me close enough to an answer to make me believe that I could escape. The only thing that I could hope for was the universe intervening to grant me freedom from this man, once and for all, and it had already left me for so long now that I doubted it was in any hurry to change that.

So I would just have to live with this. Live with Matt. And hope that one day, he would grow tired of hurting me, enough that he stopped for good.

Though I doubted I was going to be granted a reprieve anytime soon.

Chapter Two

Tommy

"SHIT!" JAKE SNARLED as he paced back and forth in front of his computer. I wanted to tell him to sit down and calm down, but I knew that would only make things worse. If there was one thing I knew about my big brother, it was that he didn't take kindly to being told what to do. And, with his fuse already as short as it was, just that would have been enough to cause a nuclear-level explosion.

"What the fuck are we going to do?" he demanded, turning his gaze on me and narrowing his eyes. It was strange, honestly – the only time that I could ever see our father in Jake was when he was pissed like this. Maybe that said something about the kind of man my father had been.

"I don't know," I replied, leaning back in my seat. "But you're going to give yourself an aneurysm stalking around like that—"

"I wouldn't have to worry if you'd taken care of it," he shot back angrily. I gritted my teeth. Tempting as it was to tell him that he was the reason that we were dealing with all of this, I knew that it wouldn't get me anywhere. He would have probably flipped the table over, and the last thing we needed were to incur any more expenses right now.

For once, Jake had a reason to be angry. Normally, he could flip at anything, even in the midst of a normal conversation, but this was different – his attitude was well-justified, and I knew that he wasn't going to drop this until he could figure out how to fix the mess that we were living in right now.

It had all started because we wanted to expand a little. Which is fine if you're running a fast-food brand or something, but it's a whole different beast when you find yourself encroaching on the territory of other mafia who aren't willing to share.

"It's what Dad would have wanted," Jake had said back when he had first floated the idea to me. I had been wary of it from the start, sure that it was going to bite us in the ass sooner rather than later.

But he would have bitten my head off if he had been reminded of that. When he was in a mood like this, he just needed someone to agree with him about everything that was going through his head. I had learned my lesson trying to hold him to account, how fucking stubborn he was and how certain that he always seemed to be of what the hell he was doing.

My father would never have put up with this kind of attitude, and he knew it. He had tried it a few times when he was still around, but it had never flown. Hell, I was pretty sure that his recklessness was the very thing that had sent us down this long rabbit hole – his inability to take a step back and figure out if this was the best thing that he could do with our time. He was always throwing himself into the next thing, the next thing, the next thing, determined to make what we had bigger and better.

Shit, would that I had been the older brother, then he would have had to listen to me. He was an idiot sometimes, but he was forceful as hell, and there was no talking him out of the bad ideas that he already had in his head.

This one, though? This one had been particularly idiotic. He had hired new runners from the usual group that we used but had changed the route to pass through territory that had never belonged to us. Territory that would see us getting right under the feet of another mafia, one that had a hell of a lot more clout in this city than us. They had sent us a message, via the beaten-to-shit body of one of our runners, and I knew that they would do worse if we dared to keep going.

But if we backed off – and Jake was distinctly aware of this – then we would look weak, and the stories would spread that we weren't going to stand our ground. And any rumors of weakness would bring people to our door looking to shake us from the territory that our father had been so careful to build up over the course of his life. If we lost that...

If we lost that, then we lost the last connection that we had to him. And I wouldn't be surprised if he rose from the afterlife to kick Jake's ass in the process.

"We need to make sure they know that we're not going to roll over and take it," Jake muttered, mostly to himself.

"And how are you going to do that?" I demanded. "When that's the only option we have right now?"

"Shut up," Jake snapped back at me. He had always resented the fact that my father had liked me more than him; he never would have said out loud that he gave a damn, but I could tell that he did. He hated that he had done everything right, in his eyes, but that it hadn't been enough to win the place he'd wanted in my father's life.

Not that it had stopped him from taking it, that was. As soon as my father had passed, Jacob had installed himself as the new head of the family, and, honestly, he could fucking have it. The thought of spending the rest of my life wrapped up in this shit, given no choice but to stick with it, didn't appeal to me. I knew that it was the family business, but that didn't mean that I approved of anything that we had done to get here.

Or wanted to be part of what came next.

If Jake kept going the way he was, however, it wasn't like we were going to be able to hang on to it much longer. We were losing money, we were losing power, we were losing influence and respect, and unless we pulled something major out of the bag soon, we were going to lose everything. Much as I might not like it, I was stubborn enough not to want someone else to take it from me.

"You should have done something," Jake continued, jabbing his finger in my direction. Typical of him. Shifting the blame and trying to make sure that he didn't have to look at what he had done, how he had fucked it up.

"I'll try next time," I growled at him, hoping that he could read the sarcasm in my voice, but he didn't seem to notice.

"You better," he muttered, and I rose to my feet. I knew that there was no point trying to get through to him when he was in this mood. I needed to get the fuck out of here, and I didn't want to waste my time trying to convince him of anything more than I already had.

"I need to go," I replied. He waved his hand at me.

"Go, go," he replied. "I need some time to think."

I stopped myself from rolling my eyes at him as I turned to the door. Think? Yeah, that was a good one. I was pretty sure that Jake hadn't been able to form one coherent thought since my father died. It had all been about building power, proving himself as some titan on the scene without once considering what might come after he made his latest bid for control in this city.

I walked the distance back to my apartment, glad for the crowds as people streamed out of their offices for the day. Sometimes you just needed to vanish into a group of people, pretend that you were nothing more than a drop of water in a giant river.

Most of the people around me would have seen me standing out like an icicle on a hot day. If anyone around me had any idea of what I did, who my family was, they would have called the cops and run for their lives. I didn't blame them. I had become inured to the mess that I was involved with, but other people were still sensitive to the violence, the pain, the inherent battle that came with having to survive here.

By the time that I arrived home, I was more irritated than when I'd left. When I was with Jake, the way he talked to me convinced me to some degree that I must have been culpable for this. But it was all his fault. I had tried to tell him to back the fuck off and give ourselves some time to make sure that we were solid in our own territory before we did anything to anyone else's.

I wasn't even sure who the hell he was trying to prove himself to. The memory of our father, maybe? Sure, but he must have known that our dad would have shot down every idea he'd come up with to expand before we had time to focus on the smaller details. He was always thinking big, too big, in too broad a stroke for anyone else to keep up with, and when the details turned out blurry as a result, he would turn on whoever was closest to him to pay the price.

Right now, that was me. And I didn't have it in me to fight him. Anyone else, yeah, sure, I would have been ready to throw down and make a scene and make sure that they knew that they couldn't talk shit and expect to get away with it. But Jake had been doing this for so long, and the two of us had ended up in so many foul battles over the shit that he would pull that I had quit fighting back.

I sank down into my couch, alone in my apartment once more. This place still didn't feel like a home to me, even though I had lived here for nearly four years – I still hadn't bothered to hang up photos, fill the cupboards with the food I liked to cook. Maybe I was hoping something else was going to change. That my life would shift and would turn into something that I actually wanted it to be.

But I couldn't rely on anyone else to deal with this shit for me. I had to handle it myself. And that meant calling Jake to account, and doing something to get him out of the mess that we were in. I knew that he must have been losing his mind right now, and leaving him in that shitty little makeshift office of his for much longer was going to push him over the edge.

I rose to my feet and headed to grab some takeout menus from where I had stuffed them in my kitchen. I needed something to eat. I needed to get out of my head for a while. I needed to be able to cut off the outside world for as long as it took to get my head clear.

I stared at the lists of food in front of me, trying to find something that sounded good. Nothing did. Everything seemed like too much, every choice more than I could handle. But I needed to step the fuck up and do what I could to keep my father's legacy alive – not let my depression get the best of me.

And that started with as much Chinese takeout as I could eat.

Chapter Three

Charlotte

"CHAR!" AMBER CALLED to me, waving wildly as she spotted me from the other side of the street. I smiled and waved back, trying to keep my face as neutral as I could.

In truth, I was feeling pretty damn good that particular morning. Pretty damn good, because I had woken up to find that my so-called fiancé still wasn't home. Whatever woman he had managed to get his hands on, she must have really been holding his attention, and I was more than fine with turning a blind eye to the fact that he wasn't home.

I made myself coffee and dropped Amber, my best friend, a quick text to ask her if she wanted to meet up. Ever since I had started planning for the wedding, I had seen a little less of her, maybe because I knew that she would be able to see through the front that I was throwing up to pretend that everything was all right, and I couldn't stand the thought of having to tell anyone what was actually happening there.

Not that she wouldn't have understood. She was part of this world just the same way that I was – that was how we'd met, actually, since I didn't know a single person out in the real world, beyond the confines of what my father did for a living. She would have listened to every word that came out of my mouth and understood what I was going through, and she would have done everything that she could to help me find a way out.

But as I applied the concealer carefully over the bruise on my jaw, I knew that I couldn't. Because if I told her, then I would have been putting her in danger, and I didn't want to do that. I needed her to be an escape from my life, not an extension of it, and I knew that if I spilled the truth to her she was going to look at me differently than I wanted her to. I needed to just be her friend, not some charity case that she needed to look out for whenever she got the chance.

Still. I was glad for the break, and I waved at her as she hurried toward me to give me a big hug. Her dark, curly hair was pulled back into a wild ponytail, and she was wearing a grin so wide that it looked like it would split her face in two.

"Okay, it's been way too long since I last saw you," she gushed. "What's been going on? How's the wedding planning going?"

"Can we grab a coffee first?" I asked her, hoping that my voice sounded light and breezy. She nodded, but a small furrow appeared in her brow.

"Of course," she replied, and she led me back to the table where a waiter was already hovering, ready to take my order. People in this part of the city knew us, and they knew that they didn't want to do anything to get on our bad side. Not that I would have been reporting the bad attitude of some random waiter to anyone, but still, at least it meant that the service was always on point.

Amber slid her hand to my arm and gave me a squeeze. My heart dropped, and I panicked, wondering if I hadn't done a good enough job of hiding the bruises and she was about to ask me about them. But instead, she offered me a smile.

"So tell me, how are things going?" she asked. "I can't believe you're actually getting married – damn, it's less than a year away now, right?"

"Yeah, less than a year," I replied, trying to keep my voice bright and upbeat. I knew that she would be able to see through me if I wasn't careful, and if she did...

"You're looking forward to it, right?" she asked. I nodded quickly.

"Oh, yeah, of course," I replied. "Just...a lot to think about, with the wedding planning and all..."

"You ever need help with that, you let me know, okay?" she replied, and I nodded again. I felt like the less I said, the better it would be, and I hated that I was keeping so much from her. Normally, the two of us were just able to talk for hours, never pausing for an instant, but I knew that I had to be careful not to give anything away right here.

She eyed me for a moment as the waiter returned to the table with my coffee and placed it in front of me. I smiled up at him in thanks, but he didn't make eye contact, sliding away the first chance he got. I knew that he wanted to vanish into the ground, and I wished that I could tell him that he had nothing to worry about with me. I wasn't going to do anything to hurt him or screw him up, and I didn't want to have people ducking and diving to avoid me out in the real world.

"You sure you're okay?" Amber asked me, lowering her voice and leaning toward me. "Everything going all right with Matthew?"

I paused for a moment. I could have just told her. I could have grabbed the wipes that I kept in my purse and scrubbed them over my face and shown her the bruise, told me that he had done that and a whole lot worse, too, and she would have been horrified but at least she would have been there to help me. At least I could be honest with someone, at least I wouldn't have to deal with this all alone any longer...

But instead, I just nodded, kept smiling. I didn't want her to worry. I didn't even know where to start if I had – where would I begin to fill her in on the mess that was going on inside my head, inside my home, when the rest of the world wasn't looking? I hated that. Hated myself for thinking about it, when I was supposed to be having fun with my friend. These were some of the only times that I got to forget what the hell was going on in the rest of my life, and I wasn't going to let myself get pulled back into the darkness again.

"Yeah, I'm all good," I replied, keeping my tone breezy. "Just a little stressed with the wedding planning, that's all. I'm going to need you to start looking at dresses with me soon…"

"Oh, I can't wait," she exclaimed, clapping her hands together. My heart twisted. I didn't want to mislead her, but what the hell else was I supposed to do? I couldn't go back and admit the truth now. I couldn't undo the happiness that I had given her, not after all of this.

"When am I going to find a man, though?" she asked, sighing and leaning back in her seat. "I feel like I need to settle down already. And I'm pretty sure that my father's going to marry me off to someone if I'm not careful…"

Suddenly, her eyes drifted to a spot behind me, and her lips quirked up into a smile. She leaned toward me conspiratorially.

"Don't look now, but there are totally a couple of cute guys checking us out right now," she murmured, raising her eyebrows playfully. I laughed.

"Well, why don't you go over to talk to them?" I asked her. "You could find out what they're up to. And with two of them, you're more likely to get a hit…"

"Hey, I could get them anyway," she protested, and she flicked her gaze back to them again. Damn, I missed that – just being able to enjoy flirting with some strangers, enjoy their attention without having to worry about Matt finding out and losing his shit on me. He could go out and spend his nights with random women, of course, but if I dared to do the same? Yeah, I was going to have to pay for it. I hated him for that. Hated him for a lot of things, actually. But that wasn't the point.

"I'm going to get them over here," she muttered, and she raised her hand. My eyes widened.

"Oh, no, don't," I pleaded with her. "If Matt finds out…"

"He's not going to. It's just talking," she laughed. She didn't know what she was putting me at risk of right now. I couldn't blame her for what she was doing, but still, it scared the hell out of me.

A moment later, they were at our table. I lowered my gaze to my coffee, not wanting to deal with any of this, but that wasn't going to scare them off quite so easily.

"Hey," one of them greeted us. I flicked my eyes up to look at him. He had a cocky air about him, a wide grin on his face as he eyed up Amber like she was a piece of meat he wanted to sink his teeth into.

"Well, hi," Amber replied, and she flipped her hair theatrically over her shoulder and fluttered her lashes at him. The other dude flashed me a brief smile, as though he was telling me that he felt just the same way that I did about all of this. I smiled back. He had a nice smile, actually, genuine and warm, and his dark eyes seemed to glisten with flecks of gold as he stood there in front of me.

"What are you two doing out here with no escort?" he remarked, trying to sound playful but coming off as a little stunted. The other dude rolled his eyes at his friend's cheesy pick-up line, and I had to stifle a chuckle. At least he wasn't quite as forward as that, which was a relief.

"We're just having some fun," Amber replied. "What about you? Who let you two out on the town?"

"Guess we just got lucky to run into you," he remarked, and his eyes flicked over to me for a moment. I didn't like the way he looked at me, as though he knew something about me that he didn't want to come clean about. I shivered and looked away from him. Maybe they recognized me. I hoped not. I hated it when people figured who I was and treated me differently. And the last thing I wanted was some other needy gangster trying to push his way into my life.

"Guess you are," Amber shot back. She had always been more confident with men than I was, and I always admired how blatant she was about her attraction to them. Even before I had gotten involved with the shittiest guy on the planet, I had never had her straightforwardness. And right now, all I wanted was for them to leave us alone, because I knew if the man I was supposed to marry found out that I had been talking to someone else, he was going to make my life a living hell.

Amber and the guy shared a little conversation before she shooed them off, seeming to notice my discomfort; the other man, the one who hadn't said much, glanced over at me as he left, and I felt a little twist in my stomach. Gosh, he really was gorgeous—not that I would be allowed to do anything about it.

"Well, today just got a lot more interesting," Amber remarked as she waved the waiter over to get us another drink. Though, right now, I felt like I could do with something stronger than a coffee or three.

Chapter Four

Tommy

JAKE DIDN'T WAIT FOR me to invite him in; as soon as he opened the door, he marched over the threshold, and I could tell from the look on his face that he had a plan.

And that he wasn't going to back off until he got a chance to put it into action.

"What are you doing here?" I asked him blearily. I had been up late last night, after I had spent the day with him, feeling irritable and irritated; I knew that I shouldn't let him get under my skin, but it was hard when all that I could think about was the mess he was making of our father's legacy.

"I've figured it out," he explained, marching back and forth in my living room like I had asked him personally to come join me.

"Figured what out?"

"How we're going to fix all of this," he explained. "How we're going to make sure that everyone takes us seriously around here and they never forget that we're a threat."

"What the fuck are you talking about—"

"You remember the girls we met yesterday?" he asked, and I nodded. I didn't like just going up to chicks and hitting on them when they hadn't made it explicitly clear that they were into it. And it was obvious to me that only one of them had been vaguely interested in either of us.

Jake was terrible at flirting, but this woman seemed willing to put up with it. I hoped that, for her sake, it wouldn't go any further than that.

Her friend had been more nervous, though. Specifically avoiding looking at either of us, as though worried about what might happen if she did. I was curious to find out why she was so freaked out, but there was no time to talk to her. Not when I was doing my best to get Jake away from that other chick before something else happened. They were just trying to have a good time together, and I wasn't going to try to force anything more out of them.

"Yeah, of course I do," I replied. "What about them?"

"That was Charlotte Saint Claire," he explained, speaking that name out loud as though it was an incantation to fix all of our problems.

"What about it?" I asked. I knew that the Saint Claires were a big deal in this city, and I knew that my father had had a few clashes with them over the years, but I didn't care about that. We kept out of their way because they could throw their weight around and cause more damage to us than we could handle.

"You know who she is, don't you?" he asked. I nodded.

"She's got more power in this city than either you or me, and she doesn't even have to do anything to hold on to it," he continued, sounding pissed. He always got this way when he was talking about people who got handed shit on a platter, normally forgetting about the fact that our father had done just that when he had passed. No way that Jake could have built all this by himself.

"And yet she's just walking around out there like it's nothing," he continued. "You know what we could do with it? You know how we could use it?"

"What are you getting at?" I asked him, furrowing my brow.

"We kidnap her," he replied, spreading his hands wide. And my jaw dropped.

"I'm sorry, what the fuck did you just say?" I shot back at him. He had to be kidding. There was no way that we could do something like that. Even thinking about it for more than a second felt like something that was going to get us both into trouble...

"You know who she's engaged to, right?" he remarked. "Matthew Golder. He's Lou Saint Claire's right-hand man, and the two of them together – they're going to pay good money to get her back once we have her."

"Yeah, and then they're going to kill us both," I reminded him. "You know that you can't fuck with people like that. What the hell are you thinking?"

"I'm thinking that we need to do something to make sure that people understand we're not to be fucked with," he explained. Not that he felt the need to give that much of an explanation. It was obvious to him that this was what needed to be done, and there was nothing that I was going to be able to do to talk him out of it.

"You're talking shit," I told him bluntly, waiting for him to hold his hands up and admit that he was wrong. I knew that he was desperate, but this was going to get us in more trouble than he could handle. I was sure of it.

"I know what I'm doing," he replied. I snorted.

"Oh, yeah?" I shot back. "And what the fuck is that? You're going to swoop in and steal her away and then just tell them that you took her, and they're going to do whatever you want?"

"Yeah, they will," he replied, and his eyes widened with excitement. "You know how these guys are about their family, especially the girls. They're protective. And they know that they can use them to form bonds with other families. They're not going to let anyone take them, and they're not going to let any damage come to them, either."

"You're talking about her like she's a fucking doll," I growled at him. I knew where his head was at, but that didn't mean that I had any more time for his bullshit right now. I couldn't stop thinking about how nervous that girl had seemed, how she had dipped her head down to let her long blond hair cover her face. She knew that when she was out in the world, she was nothing more than what people knew of her family. Likely trying to avoid my gaze because she knew what I would think of her if she actually looked at me.

"That's what you need to think about, buddy," he replied. I could tell that he wasn't going to drop this. His voice had this condescending tone that was meant to remind me that he was my big brother and that I was going to listen to him, no matter what bullshit he was spouting right now.

"Think about how much respect we're going to get for something like this," he muttered, shaking his head with excitement. "Going after the Saint Claires. Nobody's going to dare fuck with us—"

"Yeah, because we're going to be dead," I told him bluntly. "Drop it. We can't do this."

"If we don't do something big, they're going to start seeing us as weak," he pointed out. I knew he had a point. And for the life of me I couldn't think of anything more convincing than what he had come up with. If they really were willing to pay a handsome ransom, then we would be in the money, and in the most formidable bracket of gangsters in this city.

"You don't know what you're getting yourself into," I warned him. I still didn't like the idea of going through with this – yes, I knew that he was groping around, searching for anything that he could find to bring to life what he thought he had to, but that didn't mean that I was willing to just roll over and let my brother get himself into something stupidly dangerous for no good reason.

"Or maybe you just aren't on my level right now," he fired back. "You know that this makes sense. And you know that Dad wouldn't have been afraid to do something daring to get what he wanted..."

It was a dirty trick, bringing up our father like that, because he knew that I still missed him. And he knew that he had a point. My father had been willing to do a lot of things just to keep the mission that he had put into motion ticking over, and he would have taken the opportunity like this one if he had been here to do it. He knew how important it was to keep up the vision that people had of us, almost as important as it was to actually do the shit that needed to be done to keep our place in this business, and I couldn't argue with that.

"I know," I muttered. I was forcing myself to come around to the idea. How the hell would we go about it? How could we be sure that it was as safe as possible? Was there anything I could do to try and make sure that my brother didn't get killed in the process? I had no idea. He was hot-headed, unable to think about much more than what he wanted in the moment, and I got the feeling that he would have walked out of this door and cruised the city until he'd found her again, stuffed her in his car, and made a run for it.

"So you're in?" he asked, grinning triumphantly. I looked away from him. I didn't want to admit that he had a point, and I didn't want him to believe that he had my blessing to go run out of here and do something that he couldn't take back.

"As long as can talk about this first," I warned him. I could already sense the energy coming off him in waves, and I wanted to tell him to sit the fuck down and think this through before he did anything. But it would have been fruitless. I knew what Jake was like. And I knew that there wasn't much that I could do to stop it now that it was in motion.

"Shit, there's nothing to think about," he replied, waving his hand, like he was shoving the very concept away from him.

"Yes, there is," I replied firmly. "If we're going to do this, we're going to do this properly. You hear me?"

He fired a pissy look at me, and I could feel the hissy fit that he was going to through lingering around the edge of this conversation. I didn't care. He would get himself killed if he did this wrong, and I wasn't about to lose the last member of my family. Even if sometimes I wished that I could have a break from him.

"Then where do we start?" he demanded. I gestured for him to sit down. When he was on his feet like that, in his head, I knew that I couldn't get through to him, and I knew that this was the opportunity to pull him into the real world and put something into place that was going to work.

"We start with finding out as much about him as possible," I explained. "And her. Where she goes, what she does, when she does it."

"And from there?" he asked, leaning forward with interest. He really thought he was on to something here. Best I could do was moderate how stupid he was going to be about this and make sure that he came out of it alive.

"We find a way to get close to her," I explained. "We have to take it slow. Make sure that we make this as clean as we can. Make sure that we don't get her hurt, so that we can give her back to her father in one piece."

"Right, right," he muttered. I nodded. And I tried not to think about the nervous face of the girl that we were talking about kidnapping.

Chapter Five

Charlotte

AS I SAT THERE, HANDS clasped in my lap, waiting for the wedding planner to arrive, I prayed that she wasn't going to ask too many questions about why my fiancé wasn't here. Because I didn't have the answers – and I wasn't sure that I could handle the sympathetic look that I knew she was going to give me when she realized it.

We were still nine months out from the wedding, and I knew that it was normal not to have everything worked out, but normally the other half was at least supposed to be showing an interest, weren't they? Matt didn't give a shit. He didn't care what happened as long as we got married and he got to call me his. Well, call my family his, I guessed. If we got married, it would insulate him against any mistakes he might make or anything my father might do. That was all this had been about from the very start.

He didn't give a damn about me. Never had. The way he talked to me, the way he hurt me, the things he did to me – it wasn't about love. It was about work, about his job, and I was nothing more than a means to an end. I hated feeling this way, hated knowing that I had no way out, but I couldn't see a way to escape. Short of packing up my stuff and running across the country, I was stuck with him, and that was the end of it, no matter how badly I knew that I needed to get away.

And even if I ran, I knew that he and my father would track me down again. This life would always come looking for me. If it had been that easy to escape then I would have done it already, but it was anything but. This life would always catch up to you, no matter how much space you tried to put between yourself and it, and I just had to accept that.

"Oh, hello!"

I looked up to see Tracey, my wedding planner, planting herself down opposite me. I hadn't even bothered to get a table for three this time, didn't even want to keep up the pretense that Matt was going to turn up or anything. I knew that he didn't care, that he never had. He just wanted this to be over with. It was up to me, as the woman, to see it through. I couldn't wait to get this meeting over with, be able to crawl back into bed. Maybe I would even get lucky and Matt would be out with another one of his lady friends...

"Hi," I replied, trying to keep my voice perky and bright. I knew that she would start to suspect something if I was anything other than totally delighted to see her, and I didn't want to give myself away, not for a second. I knew that I had to be careful. Any wrong move, any glimmer that I didn't want to go through with this, and she might have guessed that something was wrong and reported back to the people who would use that information against me.

"It's so good to see you," she told me, and she reached into her bag and pulled out a small leather folder where she was keeping everything that we had talked about so far. I eyed it for a moment; I knew that it was still smaller than it should have been, because I hadn't come up with as many ideas as most of her clients. Not that I didn't want to, not that I didn't like the idea of putting a wedding together, but because the thought of what waited for me at the end of it was too horrible for me to face. I knew that I had to keep myself pushing forward, though, and that this meeting would be a good chance to prove that.

"Yeah, you too," I replied, and I gestured to the spot beside me where I knew Matt should have been. "Sorry about – well, you know how busy things can get..."

"Yeah, of course," Tracey agreed, smoothing her hair back from her face and nodding. "I work with a lot of clients on Wall Street; I know how crazy things can be out there. Most of the husbands-to-be I don't even get to meet until the wedding day!"

I managed to laugh. She was lucky that she wasn't going to get to know Matt, that was for sure. I got the feeling that she would sense something was off about the Wall Street story that I had spun to her when we had first met; I knew that I couldn't come clean about the truth, and I didn't much want to, either. If she found out the reality of the kind of people that she was getting involved with, I would bet that she would be out the door before I had a chance to mention cake-testing.

"So what is it you want to focus on today?" she asked. I shrugged and picked up the menu that the waiter had dropped off at our table.

"I really don't care," I replied. "Maybe just touch base with everything again? Figure out where we're going to go from here?"

"That sounds good to me," she agreed, and she started to leaf through her folder and the meeting began.

I tried to keep myself focused, but in truth, it was hard to think of anything but how much I wanted to go home, slip into a hot bath, and then go to bed. I had managed to beg Matt into giving us separate bedrooms, at least until the wedding, and I knew he preferred it that way, anyway – he probably thought that he was being totally sneaky about the women that he was bringing back to the house, even though I knew they were there and what they were getting up to. It wasn't exactly hard to guess. But maybe he just didn't give a shit whether I knew or not. He was probably certain that I couldn't do anything about it, anyway, so what was the point in trying to sneak around and pretend like he gave a damn if I found out?

I couldn't believe that I was going to have to marry that piece of shit. Of all the men I had known who had worked for my father over the years, Matt was the worst – cruel, sharp, downright mean. That was all he had going for him. He could be rough, he could do what needed to be done. And I knew that my father needed someone like that, even if I wanted to pretend that his line of work didn't involve the kind of person that Matt was.

I was trapped with him, trapped in this. I knew that I would just have to live with the horror of everything that he was going to do with me, hope that I managed to keep whatever family he forced on me out of it – shit, the thought of having children with him was enough to make me feel ill. I couldn't imagine bringing more of him into the world, even if that was what was expected of me. I knew that he was a monster and if I was to open up the rest of the world to people like him, I would be just as bad as he was. Well, not maybe just as bad, but...

But bad enough. I wanted to be able to stand up for myself, but I didn't even know where to start. My whole body ached whenever I thought about having to spend the rest of my life standing beside that man, acting as though I cared for him – acting as though he cared for me even the remotest little bit. When I knew that he was going to have dozens of women on the side over the years. He would only come home to me if he had some anger to work out, and I would have to be there to take it from him. To carry the weight of everything that he wanted to unleash on the world. That was to be my job from the moment he put that ring on my finger.

And I couldn't think of anything worse.

Tracey and I talked through everything that I had planned out already, and I wondered what sort of sick, twisted joke the universe was playing on me having to sit here and pretend that I was excited about any of this. But soon enough, the dinner was over, and I was outside on the street looking for a cab and wondering how long it would take me to get from where I was standing now to lying in a bubble bath with a glass of wine and forgetting about everything that the rest of this year was going to bring me.

My phone rang, and I answered it at once – a learned habit, from knowing that Matt would lose his shit on me if I didn't snatch up to answer him as soon as I got the chance. I started walking as I lifted it to my ear, the energy buzzing through me, needing to be worked off, even though I had no idea where I was going.

"Hi, honey," my father greeted me. I felt a wash of relief – at least it wasn't Matt.

"Hey, Daddy," I replied. "How are you?"

"I'm fine," he replied. "Are you free? I'd like to take you and Vanessa for something to eat."

"Oh, I just..." I began, initially planning to tell him that I'd already eaten and that he didn't need to worry about getting me something to eat, but I stopped in my tracks. I knew that I had to go along with this. He was trying to keep the family together, doing his best to make sure that the two of us didn't feel neglected. Vanessa was my little sister, and I didn't see much of her these days – I knew that she was jealous that I was going to be married to Matt, and I almost wished that I could tell her that she was welcome to him, but I wouldn't have wished that on anyone, let alone my sister.

"Yeah, that sounds nice," I agreed. If I went out with them, at least that guaranteed that I wasn't going to have to go back to the house again in case Matt was there. If there was a single person that he respected in this world, it was my father, and that meant that I could leverage him to prove that I was doing the right thing.

"Where are you? I'll send a car," he replied.

"It's okay, I can make my own way there," I replied. "Just tell me where it is and I'll head on down, all right?"

"All right," he replied, though he sounded reluctant. He didn't like the thought of either me or my sister wandering around alone, but I knew I had nothing to worry about. Nobody would dare do or say shit to either of us, not if they had any idea what was good for them.

"See you soon," I told him, and I hung up the phone and looked around. I was a couple of streets over from the restaurant I had been at with Tracey, and I couldn't recognize this place. Had I been here before? I looked around, trying to see anything that would tell me where I happened to be, but the place was quiet, no shops or stores or anything that might have tipped me off.

Suddenly, I heard footsteps behind me. In the quiet of this street, they made a shudder run down my spine. I started walking, hoping that whoever was following me just so happened to be on the same street as me and wasn't following me, but in a place this quiet-

And then, all at once, the world went black. I felt the rough cloth shoved over my face and hands on me, pulling me back. As my stomach dropped into my shoes, I knew that my father had been right to worry. And I knew that there was nothing he could do to help me now.

Chapter Six

Tommy

I SLIPPED INTO THE room where we had left her, flicked on the light, and gazed at the woman on the bed before me.

It was hard to believe that we had really done this. Everything had happened in such a rush that I still found myself wondering if this could actually be happening – if we could really have just snatched a woman like that off the street and made off with her. I knew that, if anyone found out that we had her, we were going to be on the wrong end of Saint Claire's entire crew, but for now, things had gone exactly how we had wanted them to.

And I felt like punching the air in victory. We'd done it. We were in the process of doing it. And I knew that nothing was going to get in my way now.

She had wandered off down the street after she'd been in that meeting with her friend – I had no idea who she was talking to on the phone, but it got her distracted enough that she managed to land herself in one of the rare quiet streets of the city, making it all the easier for us to grab her. Jake had tossed her phone and her purse on to the sidewalk, and I had shoved the bag over her head, getting her into the van, where Jake had dosed her with a tranquilizer to knock her out. She had been in so much shock that she'd hardly had a second to respond, hardly even begun to fight back. She didn't get a proper look at me, so she wouldn't have time to recognize me. Not yet, anyway.

We had brought her to our house out in Tuxedo, the one that our father had left us. It was a huge place, but not many people knew about it – unless you happened to know our uncle, you would never think to look here for us. Which was what we needed right now. Somewhere to lay low and let the tension build back in the city about what had happened to her. I knew that people would be starting to worry, and that was just the way we needed it. We needed them second-guessing, going back on themselves, wondering what they could have missed. So by the time that we decided to come clean about what we had done and asked for what we wanted in return for her safety, they would be willing to hand it over without a second thought.

She must have been scared shitless before we put her out. The thought kindled some regret and guilt inside of me, but I pushed it down. I knew that with how she'd grown up she would be able to handle this. This was nothing compared to the things her family had done.

Slowly, I watched as her eyes fluttered open once more. She had been out for nearly ten hours now, and it was morning again. I hadn't been able to sleep, too worried that she was going to up and run out on us the first chance she got, even though Jake had assured me that he was going to do everything he needed to in order to ensure that didn't happen.

She looked around, bleary, not lifting her head from the pillow – and then, all at once, she started upright, her voice catching in her throat as she tried to let out a cry of fear.

"What the fuck is going on?" she demanded, her eyes widening as they locked on to mine. Gone was the woman who had been too scared to look at me when we had first run into her and her friend – she was clearly pissed, and I wasn't surprised. Scared, too. Wondering what we were going to do with her, why she had woken up still alive and what we wanted with her now.

"Calm down," I said, taking a step towards her. She pulled back from me, pressing herself against the headboard as though she was trying to pass through it to the wall behind her.

"Don't tell me to calm down," she shot back, her voice tinged with anger and hurt. "What the hell am I doing here? Who are you? What do you want with me?"

"You're safe," I promised her. "We're not going to do anything to hurt you, as long as you can keep quiet and stay calm."

"Oh, you think I'm not going to make a fuss?" she demanded, her eyebrows shooting up. She tipped her head back and let out a cry. The sound echoed around us, filling the room. If there had been anyone around for a mile, it might have spooked me, but as it was, I couldn't help but laugh.

"What the hell are you doing?" I asked, cutting her off.

"I'm yelling for help," she fired back at me. Her eyes were blazing with anger, and I knew that she was going to take a chunk out of me if I got any closer to her. I didn't blame her. This was a woman who hadn't had to deal with anything serious in her entire life, and now here we were, having grabbed her off the street and brought her to the ass-end of nowhere. Of course she was pissed. Probably missing her latest shopping trip with her girlfriends for this.

"There's nobody around to hear you," I told her. "Just rest, okay? We're not going to do anything to you—"

"As long as you play by the rules."

I turned around to see Jake standing in the doorway. His face was twisted with anger, and I knew that he hated the woman sitting in front of us. He would never have come out and said it, but I knew that it was true – he looked at her and saw everything that he thought he should have had, all the things that he believed should have come easy to him. A connection to a powerful family, being part of a world that she didn't seem to realize the importance of. He would never have that, no matter how hard he tried. The best that he could hope for was to exploit her importance in her world to get enough cash to ensure that we were safe for the foreseeable future.

"And what are the rules?" she demanded, glancing over at my brother. I could see the flash of fear in her face as she looked to him. She could sense that he wasn't like me – could sense that he wasn't going to be as kind as I had been. I didn't blame her for her fear. She didn't understand just how much he was willing to do, how far he was willing to go.

"The rules are you stay quiet, keep your head down, and nothing bad is going to happen to you."

"And if I don't want to do that?" she asked.

"Do I really have to tell you what we'll do?" Jake replied harshly. He didn't want to say it out loud, but I knew that he would kill her if he had to. The thought of seeing the life snuffed out of this woman, no matter whose daughter she was, didn't sit right with me – but I just had to hope it would never come to that.

She slumped back against the bed and lifted her gaze up to the ceiling. I could tell that she was still wracking her brains on how to get out of here.

"You know who my father is?" she shot back at him. "You know what he'll do to you when he finds out that you took me?"

"Of course we know who your father is," Jake fired back at her. "Why do you think you're here? You're everything we need right now. And your father is going to be the one to give it to us. Well, if he wants to get his little girl back in one piece, that is."

And with that, he turned on his heel and marched out of the room, slamming the door behind him. Great, petulance. That's what we needed right now. We were supposed to be making sure that this girl was spooked by us, scared enough to play by our rules, and Jake was acting like a teenager who hadn't gotten his way.

She looked to me again, her eyes searching mine. Slowly, she tipped her head to the side and spoke again.

"You're...the guy from the café, right?" she asked me. I nodded. "Yeah, I am."

"How long have the two of you been planning this?" she asked. I sighed. I wasn't going to give her any more answers than I had to. Spilling more than I had to would just let her get one over on us, make it easier for her father to track us down when it came to her release. I wasn't going to make it easier than it needed to be.

"It doesn't matter."

"Yes, it does," she snapped back. She was papering over her panic with anger, and I got that. She must have been pissed as hell. She was used to living her normal, comfortable little life, a life where she didn't have to worry about anything, and here we were, having pulled her right out of it and dumped her in the middle of what most people would consider a nightmare. I didn't blame her for freaking out. I knew what it must have looked like to her and I didn't much feel like trying to convince her otherwise.

"Get some rest," I told her bluntly. "You're going to need it."

"What are you talking about?" she demanded. She was spikier around the edges than I had thought she'd be. She had been so shy when we had run into her with her friend that I couldn't help but wonder what the hell was really going on there. But I could figure that out as I went – for now, I knew that I just had to make sure that she didn't get outside of this room. Even if nobody in Tuxedo would have known who the hell she was, I wasn't going to make it any easier for her to make a break for it.

Because we had come this far already. And there was no way in hell that I was going to back off now. Not when the answer to all of our problems was sitting right there in front of me.

Chapter Seven

Charlotte

AS I LAY THERE, TUCKED up under the covers, knees pulled protectively up to my chest, my stomach growled loudly.

I hadn't eaten since my meeting with Tracey the night before, and I wasn't sure that I even would have been able to swallow a mouthful of food as it was. I was terrified. Stressed out of my mind. I felt like I needed to curl up and go to sleep and forget that any of this was happening in the first place. Because there was no way in hell that someone would have been stupid enough to think that they could get away with kidnapping me. Right?

Right. The guys who had grabbed me had to be downright insane if they thought that anything good was going to come of this. I was sure that my father would have mobilized his whole force to find me again, along with Matt...

Matt. I couldn't stop wondering if this had been his doing. It seemed like the sort of thing that he would have pulled off just to make sure that he didn't have to go through with marrying me. Get me plucked off the street by some thugs, get them to take me to the middle of nowhere and spin a story about how they needed me for this or that, and then have me killed off to be certain that he would look like the victim in all of this. I wasn't sure that my father would believe him, but he knew that my dad wouldn't cast a so-called grieving member of the family out. He would still be sealed to them, just without having to deal with the irritation of keeping me around.

I was trying not to think about what these men might want from me. I couldn't stop thinking about the first time I encountered them, out with Amber – I wondered if she had any idea of this. If she had been flirting with that other one, the older one, because she had been in cahoots with them all along...

But I knew that my best friend would never have done something like that to me. Not in a million years. She was far kinder than that, far more loving than most of these fuckers ever would be. If there was a single person in the world that I trusted to look out for me first and foremost, it was her. I knew that she would never have let this happen.

And that meant that I was out here on my own. And I had no idea what to make of that.

I didn't even have a clue where I was in the world right now. I wished that I could just call up some sort of memory of where they had taken me, just a glimpse of what had been happening outside the windows of that van that they had bundled me into the back of, but I wasn't going to get so lucky. They had forced some pill into my mouth, and everything after that had been a blur, until I had woken up to the other one looking at me from the doorway.

I didn't know where I was or how long they were going to keep me here or anything at all that might have come in useful in getting out of this mess, but I was going to have to find a way to deal with that. There was no way out of it, no way through it, no way to get past it except to deal with what I was faced with right now. My whole body was aching from lying still for so long, and I knew that if I didn't eat something soon, I wasn't even going to be able to stand up without keeling over.

I felt gross. I needed a shower. I didn't even know if they would let me have one. The place they were keeping me in was actually pretty nice, but that didn't mean that they were going to let me use any of the facilities. This wasn't exactly a spa weekend, after all...

Suddenly the door opened opposite me, and I pushed back the covers so I could see who it was. It was the younger one again, this time, carrying a bag with what I assumed from the smell had food in it.

"How are you feeling?" he asked me. It was almost enough to make me believe that he cared. I let out a snuffle of irritation and flipped over and away from him. But the savory smell of the food floating from that bag was enough to make my stomach growl again, louder this time.

"I brought you something to eat," he told me, and I felt the weight of him as he sat down on the end of the bed. I looked over at him. He was holding out the bag to me, and I didn't have it in me to turn it down. I reached out and snatched it from him, pulled it open, and grabbed the toasted sandwich inside, taking a huge bite of it before I could stop myself, and then another. It was greasy and hot and cheesy, and I was so ravenous that I was practically swallowing bites whole without chewing.

"Hey, hey, slow down," he warned me. "You don't want to choke."

I glanced up at him. Much as I wanted to tell him to go fuck himself and that he didn't get a say in how I ate my damn food, I knew that he was right. I didn't want to choke, because if I did, that meant that he was going to have to touch me, and I knew that I wasn't going to be able to deal with the way that made me feel. I slowed down, chewing, pulling my knees up to my chest again protectively to make sure that he couldn't get any closer than he already had.

"How are you doing?" he asked me. The concern in his voice sounded real, but I knew better than to believe it for a single second. I knew that he just needed me in one piece to carry out his part of the plan, whatever that happened to be. I would figure it out soon enough.

"I'm fine," I shot back. "I need a shower, though. Can I take one?"

He paused for a moment, clearly trying to work out if this was some cunning bid of mine to make sure that I could get out. After a moment, he nodded.

"I'll need to watch you, though," he replied. I felt my cheeks flush. He really thought that I was going to just stand by and let him...let him watch me undress?

But then, it wasn't like I had much of a choice but to go along with what he was suggesting right now. I wasn't exactly a fan of it, but shit, maybe it was for the best. If that was what it was going to take to get him to accept that I wasn't going to try and make a break for it, then fine. Nothing sexual about it.

"Sure," I replied, shrugging as though I had expected that. He nodded.

"Okay," he agreed. I finished up my food and got to my feet.

"Where is it?" I asked. I could feel my stomach grumbling happily, glad to have finally been fed – well, at least some part of me was satisfied in all of this.

"Wait here," he told me, and he rose to his feet and headed out of the room again. I stood there, waiting for him to return, and wrapped my arms around myself tightly. I still didn't know how any of this was going to turn out, but I knew that I had to play by their rules for now, for as long as it took for this to be over. At least they didn't seem intent on finishing me off right then and there.

And at least I didn't have to worry about Matt walking through the door in a bad mood ready to take it out on me when I was least expecting it. That had to count for something...

A moment later, he returned, carrying a towel that he tossed to me, then jerked his head to a door that led off the room that we were in.

"Here," he told me. He wasn't a man of many words, that was for sure. Good. Because I didn't have much to say to him. I didn't want to make friends; I wanted to get out. Wanted to get out of this place and back to reality. I still wasn't sure who they were working for, but I knew that, whoever it happened to be, my father would get to the bottom of it and make sure that they paid for everything that they had done to me.

He followed me into the bathroom, and I stood there for a moment in front of the small shower stall and tried to work out what to do next. I knew that I was going to have to undress, but could I do it behind the frosted glass of the stall? Maybe, but it was so tiny that I doubted I would have had room to take all my clothes off, and I would have had to open it again to toss them all out anyway.

I looked at him again, hoping that he might show an inch of embarrassment and leave me to get changed myself, but he didn't. I supposed that there was a lot riding on him being able to keep an eye on me. He wasn't about to let me just slip through his fingers, not when they had likely spent such a long time making sure that they could get their hands on me in the first place.

Fine. I didn't have anything to be ashamed of here. I started to peel off my clothes, keeping my eyes fixed on the wall opposite me. I could feel him looking at me, but I didn't give a damn. I kept focused on the shower, promising myself that I would be in and out and dressed again in no time at all. As soon as I was done, this would be over, and maybe they would trust me enough to let me get washed up without a damn chaperone next time.

And even though there was this strange man right there watching me, I didn't feel as panicked or exposed as I should have. Maybe because I knew that he wouldn't lay a hand on me. Maybe because I understood that he needed me in one piece, and that he didn't dare hurt me.

And that was more than I could say for the man who was supposed to be marrying me, that was for sure. I reached inside the stall and turned on the water, letting it rush over my hand and warm me up. Okay, I could do this. I slipped inside and pulled the door shut behind me, tipping my head back and letting the rush of warm water slide all over my body.

Even though I knew that there was someone waiting just beyond that door for me, I didn't care. I had to stick it out for as long as I was here, and I didn't know how long that was going to be. If this was all that it took, then I could cope with it. I could manage for now.

Maybe more than manage. Because I wasn't going to have to deal with Matt for at least a little while longer. And that seemed like damn near a vacation compared to the life I had been living.

Chapter Eight

Tommy

"EVERYONE'S TALKING about it," Jake announced as he paced back and forth in front of the blazing fireplace that I had built up for us this evening. It had been such a long time since my uncle had actually lived here that the heating wasn't working as well as it should have, but luckily, I knew how to keep us warm.

"And that's a good thing?" I asked. Jake nodded.

"Means that they're going to be even more impressed when they find out who pulled this off," he replied, jerking his head in the direction of the room that she was currently locked in. It felt like the memory of her presence was burning at the back of my mind, the shock of it more than I could take. She was here. She was really here. We had really done it.

And now, we really had to handle what came next.

"How do you know they're talking about it?" I asked. As far as I knew, my brother hadn't had any contact with the outside world, and I knew that we were going to need to keep our heads down if we were going to get through this.

"I've have people back in the city keeping an eye on things for me," he explained. "Seems like they've already worked out that she's gone. They're looking for her, though I doubt they're going to think of coming all the way out here if they can avoid it..."

"Yeah, sure," I muttered. I didn't like the thought of us being on other people's radars like that. Where I could, I preferred to keep my head down. Because I knew that coming to the attention of the wrong people in this city was enough to get you killed.

Or worse.

"Everything's going just how I wanted it to," he explained, speaking quickly and sounding as delighted as I had ever heard him. I knew that he was running on fumes right now. He hadn't gotten any sleep since we had taken her and had hardly eaten anything, either. He had been checking in on her regularly, and she had mostly been either sleeping or pretending to sleep that entire time. Couldn't blame her. If I was in her position, I doubted that I would want to have conversations with the people who had stolen me away from my life.

"What are you going to do next?" I asked. Frankly, I was getting pretty sick and tired of my brother, and I wanted nothing more than for him to fuck off for a while and let me get some rest.

"I'm going to head back to the city and keep an eye on things there myself," he explained. "Make sure that it's all going just how we want it to. I need to make sure that they're really looking for her, that they really want her back, before we actually give them the option to get her again."

"Right, right," I agreed. Thank fuck. So he was going to be out of my hair for a while. I would take that. I would take anything I could get right about now – I just needed him out of here, for good, and I could get on with the rest of my life.

"You think you can handle watching her all by yourself?" he asked. I nodded.

"I know I can," I replied. "She's just a girl. She's not going to cause us any trouble."

"Yeah, that's right, she's not," he repeated, and there was an edge to his voice that told me he was trying to convince himself as much of that as he was me. "Anyway. I should get out of here—"

"Can you stay to watch her for a few hours while I get some rest?" I asked him, yawning. "I don't want to be exhausted if I'm the only one here to keep an eye on her."

"Sure, sure," he replied, distracted. I knew that he was so buzzing with energy that he wouldn't be able to get any sleep as it was. And I needed some time to myself. Sooner rather than later.

I sloped off to my bedroom, the one next to hers, and pulled the door tight shut behind me. In truth, there was another reason that I needed to be alone right now. And it had everything to do with what I had seen when Charlotte had slipped into the shower right in front of me.

Truth be told, I hadn't expected her to go through with actually getting undressed when I had been right there. I was sure that she would tell me that she was fine, that she could go without a shower, but she didn't seem to have a second thought about stripping down and slipping into the stall with me standing right there.

I had done my best to give her the dignity she deserved, but I couldn't ignore her reflection in the mirror opposite us as she stripped off. She didn't seem to have any hang-ups about getting bare-ass naked right in front of me. Maybe it was a power thing for her, proving that I didn't have any control over her or what she decided to do. Either way, she was downright gorgeous, and it was hard not to think about the way her stunning body had looked as she was getting undressed.

I lay down in bed and stared at the ceiling, trying not to let my mind float back to the way she had looked in the light of that bathroom. Her body was slim and willowy, her hips curvy and her waist so small that I felt like I could have wrapped my fingers the whole way around it – she was hot in that classic way that so few people could actually pull off, hot in a way that made it impossible to think of anything but getting my hands on her.

I slipped my hand down to my pants and unzipped, taking my already-stirring cock into my hand and beginning to stroke it as I thought of her. Damn, she was so fucking sexy. Not just the way that she looked but the way that she carried herself, the confidence with which she moved. Even behind the frosted glass of the shower, I could make out the soft sway of her body as she cleaned herself up, the way she moved this way and that like she had nothing at all to fear or be ashamed of. I liked that. Liked it a whole hell of a lot. Liked the way it made me feel, liked the way she looked when she did that, liked the soft hum that she sang to herself as she washed.

I had been itching to slide into the shower right along with her the whole time she was in there. Feel her glistening wet skin against mine, run my hands over her hips and her waist. Sink my fingers into her and see the way she reacted, see how she responded to my touch. When she had climbed out of the shower and reached for the towel, I had seen a glimpse of her nipples – pink, perky, swollen – and I could almost imagine how they could have felt between my lips, how her skin would have tasted beneath my mouth.

I moved my hand over my cock harder than before, stroking as I thought about everything that I wanted to do to her. No, not just what I wanted to do to her, but everything that I wanted her to want me to do to her. I wanted her to kiss me back and beg me for more, to take my hands and put them at those points of her body she wanted me to explore – I wanted to feel her gasp with excitement as I sank my fingers into her ass or slipped my hand between her legs to play with her eager pussy. I hadn't caught a glimpse of what she looked like down there, but I knew she would be perfectly pink and pretty, glistening with wetness from the shower and from how much she wanted me...

At least in my imagination. She was so close to me, just in the next room, and I could so easily have risen to my feet and gone to her – looked at her again, taken her in. And maybe she would have opened her arms to me, asked me to join her. I could slide into bed next to her, move inside of her, feel her lips around my cock as I thrust deep into her. Watch the way her eyes glazed with desire as she got closer and closer to the edge. I wanted to make her come. I wanted to hear the sound she made when she finished, the way she cried out when she came. I wanted to send more pleasure through her body than she had ever felt before in her life.

I closed my eyes and focused on the thought of her coming with my cock inside of her – I could almost see it, how her pretty face would screw up for a moment before she let out this cry of pleasure, her whole body tensing against mine. She wouldn't be able to hold back, wouldn't be able to hide it. She wouldn't want to, not for an instant. And I would do everything I could to make the most of it, slamming myself inside of her over and over again until I could finish, balls-deep inside her slick little pussy, filling her with my seed, making her mine for good.

And it was with that image in my head that I came, hard, alone in my bed – thinking of her, thinking of how much I wanted her. As soon as the orgasm hit me, it was followed by a wave of exhaustion, tiredness from trying to keep my head up for as long as I had been. I flopped back on to the pillow behind me and tried not to think about how shocked she would be if she had found out what I had been doing in here while she was sleeping. I knew that she was likely disgusted by me, and honestly, I couldn't say that I blamed her after what Jake and I had done.

But that didn't mean that she wasn't sexy as hell or that I could just push down my attraction to her. And that didn't mean that I had to do anything to pretend that I didn't notice how damn sexy she was. As long as I didn't hurt her, nothing else mattered.

I closed my eyes, and just before I let the tiredness take me completely, I wondered what it would have been like to fall asleep with her right there beside me. It had been a long time since I had slept next to someone else, and I would have liked to wake up next to her gorgeous form.

But I knew clearer than anything that I was the last person that she wanted to be near right now. And if I was going to get her out of this without any further harm, I was going to have to accept that.

Chapter Nine

Charlotte.

"HEY."

I woke up to the sound of a voice beside me. My eyes fluttered open – and locked on to the man who had taken me, the younger one, his hand on my shoulder as he woke me up.

"Hey," I muttered, rubbing a hand over my face, too exhausted to think about pushing him off or telling him to leave me alone. I wasn't sure that it would have worked anyway. He had kidnapped me, after all, and kidnappers weren't exactly known for being easy to debate with.

"You want something to eat?" he asked.

I nodded. I was hungry again already. How long had I been asleep? After I had gotten out of the shower, I had put my clothes on and lain down in the bed and had passed out before I could stop myself. Probably the weight of everything that had happened weighing down on me. All that adrenaline, all that fear...

Or maybe it was the lack of it. The fact that I didn't have to worry about Matt storming through the front door and telling me that I had done some indiscernible thing wrong and that I was going to pay for it. I was always on edge back home, always ready to fight for myself, but here, I didn't have to. And there was something of a relief about all of that, even though I knew it was crazy.

"You can come downstairs to eat, if you want," he told me as I straightened up and pushed the covers back. Thank goodness I'd slept with clothes on, because the thought of this man seeing me naked again – well, he would start to think that I was doing it on purpose, and I didn't want to give him that idea.

Right?

"Oh, okay," I replied. I didn't know what to make of the new freedom that was suddenly being brandished in my direction. Was it a trap? A trick? Maybe. But I didn't want to be cooped up in this room any longer than I already had been, so I nodded and climbed out of bed.

He led me out of the bedroom that I had been shut in, and I paused for a moment at the top of the stairs to gaze out of the window on to the grounds below. My jaw dropped. Just how big was this place? It wasn't like I was a strange to big, fancy houses, but most of the places my father kept were more modern than this – penthouses, stuff like that. This place seemed like a whole-ass castle. It was beautiful, actually. And I would have enjoyed the chance to explore it a little further if I hadn't been taken here and kept against my will.

"You coming?" he asked me, standing halfway down the stairs and looking up at me expectantly. I quickly followed him down. I didn't want to piss him off.

The kitchen was bigger than practically the entire top floor of the house that I had already seen, and it was laid out with breakfast food that looked like it could have come from the pages of a food styling magazine. I cast my eye over it, unable to keep the smile off my face.

"Did you make all of this yourself?" I asked him. He shook his head.

"Oh, no way," he replied, snorting with amusement, as though the mere thought of it was enough to tickle him. "We have a chef here. Most of the time he lives with Jake back in the city, but he's out here for now, while we are."

"You have a chef?" I asked, raising an eyebrow. Okay, so these guys weren't exactly poor, then. Or at least, the person who had set them up with all of this wasn't. He nodded.

"Yeah, have for years in this place," he replied as he went to start loading up his plate with food. My eyes darted to the archway that led out to what I assumed was the entrance hall to this place. I could have made a run for it. But in truth, I didn't think I would get very far. And I didn't really want to make a run for it, if I was being honest. I knew that he would catch up with me. And I knew that what would be waiting on the other side might not be much better than what I was facing right now. I didn't like the thought of it, of just getting out and leaving, not when I had no clue where I even was. I needed to keep my wits about me. I needed to make sure that I didn't let my nerves get the better of me.

"Has this place been in your family for a long time?" I asked, trying to keep my voice breezy. Honestly, it felt a little odd to be talking to him like this. He was the man who had kidnapped me, after all, and I knew that he might be willing to do more to me if I wasn't careful. But there was something about him that put me at ease, something that told me that I didn't have anything to fear from him, and I knew that the more I understood about him and why he had done this, the easier it would be to work out what was going on here. He nodded.

"Yeah, it used to belong to my father, and it's been ours since he died," he replied. "Me and my brother, I mean."

"That other guy, he's your brother?" I asked.

"Yeah, Jake," he responded. I saw a tension to his jaw, and he shook his head, like he didn't much enjoy thinking about him. Interesting. Really interesting.

"And you?" I asked. "What about you?"

"What about me?"

"What's your name?" I asked. He stared at me for a moment, surprised, clearly wondering how we had managed to get this far without sharing names with each other. This man had seen me naked, after all, and I didn't even know what he was called. But then he seemed to come to his senses.

"Tommy," he replied. Tommy – it almost seemed too sweet and too old-fashioned a name for someone like him, but I reminded myself that I didn't know this man at all. I needed to keep my wits about me. He might not even have been telling me his real name, doing his best to keep his identity a secret from me in case I got out and was able to fill in the people back in my real life on who he was and what the hell he was doing.

"Tommy," I replied. "I guess you already know who I am, right?"

"Yeah," he agreed as he took a bite of the buttered toast that was sitting out for us. I started to gather some food for myself too. I didn't know how long it was going to be before I got to eat again, and I knew that I had to take advantage of this while I still could.

"Hmmm," I muttered. I didn't know what else to say to him. I knew that there was a whole hell of a lot on my mind, but I wasn't sure where to start. And I wasn't sure what he would have told me, anyway – or how much of it would turn out to be the truth when all was said and done.

"Where's your brother?" I asked. "Is he still here?"

He shook his head.

"No, he's gone," he replied. "Back in the city. Taking care of business."

I opened my mouth again, intending to ask him what that business might have been, but I realized that I was stupid to think for a second that he would tell me.

"Oh, okay," I replied, wracking my brain to try and come up with an answer to that question. Maybe keeping an eye on the rest of my family? Shit, I doubted that Matt would even have noticed that I was gone yet – he'd probably be glad that he didn't have to worry about me for a while, glad that he didn't have to pretend to care about the wedding or about hiding his exploits with other women from me. Not that I gave a damn about that, not really. As long as he was far away from me, I didn't care where he was. I supposed on some level he already knew that.

I grabbed a croissant from the pile of food and took a big bite of it, eyeing Tommy from the other side of the room. There was something about him, something strange that I couldn't quite put my finger on. He didn't scare me, even though I knew he should. He had already shown what he was capable of doing when he had kidnapped me. But he wasn't laying a hand on me that I didn't want him to, and I couldn't remember the last time I had been around a man my age who hadn't done that to me. It was almost a little...exciting, knowing that I didn't have to fear for myself like that.

And what the fuck did that say about the man that I was supposed to go back to? What the hell did it say about the marriage that I was getting into? That I shouldn't be doing it, I was sure of that. But as soon as they got me out of here – as soon as I was back to reality, the reality that I was still stuck being a part of, whether I liked it or not – I was going to have to sit there and be pretty and make sure that I didn't let anyone else see my bruises.

Speaking of. I touched the one that had been on my jaw, feeling exposed now that I couldn't cover it up with makeup as I usually did. I didn't like that. Didn't like feeling so...out in the open like that. I hoped that they thought they had done it to me, because the notion of having to explain that they had been gentler with me than the man that I was supposed to marry was enough to make me feel a little ill. Having a little distance from the situation only brought it home even more how fucked-up this all was. I hated this. Hated myself for letting it get as far as it had. And hated more than anything that I still couldn't be honest with anyone about this.

I wondered if he was confused by how calm I was. If he thought it was strange that I was acting so cool about everything. I knew that it must have seemed insane to him that someone in the situation that I was in right now would be anything other than kicking and screaming and begging with everything that they had to get out, get out, get out.

But for now, I felt safer than I had in a long while. I knew that it might not stay like that. And I knew that things might change sooner rather than later. But for now – for now, I was going to take everything I could get, I was going to eat my breakfast, and I was going to try to absorb every little part of being with a man who actually didn't want to hurt me. He might have stolen me away from my life – but given how shitty my life had been up until that point, I wasn't going to go blaming him for ruining it.

Especially not when he was looking at me the way he was right now. Especially not when he smiled.

Chapter Ten

Tommy

WHEN JAKE CAME BACK from the city, he had a swagger in his step that told me I had something to be worried about.

Because my brother never went about anything in the way that I would have. And if he came back from New York acting the big man, then that meant that I likely had a reason to be nervous.

"How did it go?" I asked him as he strode straight into the kitchen to get himself a drink. He didn't answer until he had a scotch in his hand and had taken a long sip of the alcohol to get his shit together.

"It went perfectly," he replied, grinning widely at me as he finally got around to giving me the answer.

"And how is perfectly?" I asked him. I needed to know what we were dealing with here, if there would be anyone tracking us down.

"Lou's looking for her," he explained. "And he knows that there's a ransom. Knows that she hasn't just made a run for it by herself."

"Well, obviously," I replied. I could only imagine the kind of decadence that she lived in back in the city – I doubted that anyone would want to give that up if they had a choice.

"Did you talk to him?" I asked. I wanted to be the one who spoke to Lou, but I knew that Jake saw this whole thing as his operation and didn't want to let anyone else get in the way. He had come up with the idea for this, and he would be damned if he let anyone else take control.

"Yeah, I did," he replied, an edge of boastfulness to his voice.

"And does he know it was us?" I asked. I prayed that he hadn't been dumb enough to give that much away – I knew that Lou Saint Clare would be on our asses as soon as he got the chance, and I hoped that my brother hadn't just handed him the keys to the case.

"Of course he does," Jake replied, wrinkling his nose up at me as though I was stupid for even asking him a question like that. "He needs to know who's in control here."

"Shit," I muttered.

"What?" he snapped back. "He has to know who he's dealing with. That's how this works. Then he understands who he has to give the money to—"

"He's not going to just hand over the cash and pretend that none of it ever happened," I pointed out to my dumbass brother. "He's – shit, you have to see how crazy this is. He'll send people after us."

"He doesn't even know where we are," Jake replied. I sighed. I guessed that was a point.

"And who's he going to send, the cops?" he asked. "He knows that if he sends his own men out here, people are going to notice that he doesn't have his defenses in place back home. He's not going to risk that. There's nobody he can use to get her back. He has to play by our rules."

"Oh, yeah, like he doesn't have a dozen dirty cops on his payroll right now," I shot back. "You know that he has to be paying off all those guys to make sure that he can fight it if something like this does happen."

"I don't think so," Jake muttered back. He didn't sound sure. I knew that this wasn't what he had wanted from me, but if he really believed that I was just going to hold my hands up and let him act like he had managed to pull this all off when he had really just put us in more danger, he was crazy.

"He could have them scattered over the city right now," I snapped at him. "Come on, you have to know that. They could be looking for us. And you gave him the exact names of the people that he had to be looking for."

"Shut up," Jake snarled back at me. He hated when I talked to him like this – hated it because he knew that I had every right in the world to be pissed at the mess that he had landed us in. I didn't know what it was going to take for his foolish ass to get it through his head that we needed to be as subtle as possible, but hell, I would do everything it took to make that happen. From this point forward, I was going to be the one who went out there and took care of everything in the city since clearly, Jake couldn't be trusted to do anything close to it.

"What about the girl?" he asked, turning it on me. "You manage to keep her here, at least?"

"Of course I did," I replied. "She's been fine."

"Fine?" he asked, looking surprised. Honestly, I knew that he had a reason to be. After everything that had happened, after literally snatching her up off the street, the last thing that I had expected was for her to seem as calm as she had in the face of everything that we had been doing, but she was.

I had given her free roam of the house, pretty much allowed her to do anything that she wanted to as long as she didn't try to make a break for it. And she hadn't – she really hadn't. She had just been wandering around, sleeping and eating and showering as though this was some luxury hotel that she had come to of her own accord. She didn't seem in any rush to get out of there, and honestly, I was starting to wonder what the hell was going on there. Why didn't she want to leave? What was it back in the city that she seemed so happy to be away from?

"Yeah, she hasn't caused any trouble," I replied. "Which is more than I can say for you. We need to tighten security around here, make sure that the guys on the edges of the property keep an eye on everything and make sure that we get notice of anyone getting close to this place. Okay?"

Jake didn't reply as he turned to stalk away, but he didn't have to. He knew that I was right. He had been stupid in spilling what he had to the guys back in the city, and now we were going to have to pay the price for what he had done. It might not be easy, but we were in this mess now, and we had no choice but to see it through and hope that we could get something useful out of the other side of it.

"Is everything all right?"

Her small voice caught me off guard. I turned to see her, Charlotte, standing there right behind me. I didn't know how long she had been lurking there, but she looked concerned. What for? Surely, she should have been glad that she had heard the two of us talking, annoyed with one another? I didn't know what to say to her. I just needed to come out with something.

"It's fine," I replied, and I marched out of the kitchen and back into the house. I had things to think about, shit to pull together, since my brother had decided that it would be a good idea to go swinging his dick all over the city. Now that Lou knew who we were and what we were doing, there would be all the more reason to step up our security and make sure that nobody got close to the house.

"What's going on?" she asked me as she followed behind me with interest. I had to say, I was still pretty surprised that she hadn't made a break for it. She must have seen the security around the house, known that there was no way that we were going to let our meal ticket out that easy, but still. She almost seemed comfortable here. Happy, even. At peace.

"Nothing that concerns you," I replied.

She laughed. "Doesn't it all concern me right now?" She sounded more amused than anything else. I stopped in my tracks and turned to her. Something about the way that she was looking at me right now drew something out of me, something that I should have known better than to indulge.

"Why haven't you run?" I asked her. She met my gaze steadily, as though she had been expecting me to ask her that question since she had arrived.

"I haven't yet, have I?" she pointed out. "Isn't that all that matters?"

"Yeah, but why?" I pressed her.

She didn't have an answer to that one, and it only made me even more curious to know what the heck she was keeping from me right now. I knew that there had to be something, and I would have been lying if I'd said that I wasn't curious to find out just what it might have been.

"It doesn't matter," she replied. "Just...I haven't yet."

"Yet being the operative part," I answered her coolly. She didn't have anything to say to that. She knew that I was right. She was counting down the seconds until she could really make a break for it. I didn't know why she hadn't taken advantage of how lax I had been up until this point. Maybe there was a part of me, a part of me that I would never have admitted to existing in a million years, that wanted her to get up and run from me. Wanted her to get as far from here as possible, because that would have meant that I wouldn't have to deal with the mess that my brother had made.

Maybe. Or maybe I liked having her around for reasons that I couldn't quite put into words yet.

"What about your fiancé?" I asked her. I had seen the ring shining on her finger, and I knew from the grapevine that she was due to be married to her father's right-hand man—a typical move used to solidify him into the family for good. She shrugged.

"What about him?" she replied. She seemed to be almost daring me to ask more about him, to find out what I could about the truth that she seemed so willing to share with me, but honestly, I didn't think that she was ready to tell me everything yet. Not quite yet.

My phone rang, giving me an easy out of the conversation, and I glanced at her. I felt the urge to apologize for cutting things off so abruptly between us, but instead, I just turned away to take the call. I wasn't sure what it was about her that made me feel as though I owed her an apology, but I wasn't going to give in to it. Just because she was here, just because she happened to be trapped in this house with me, didn't mean that I had to charm her. She was supposed to be our prisoner.

So why was it that she was acting like our guest?

Chapter Eleven

Charlotte

AS I SAT ON THE EDGE of the bed, staring out of the small window that looked up to the night sky above me, I felt so fucking guilty I could hardly control myself.

I felt guilty for leaving everyone. And yes, I knew that I had hardly made the choice to get out of the city like that. I had been picked up off the street by a couple of low-level criminals who were trying to make a name for themselves, or something like it. I still wasn't entirely sure what their game plan was, but I knew that I was stuck in the middle of it, and that I would have to play along for the time being to make sure that nothing bad happened to me.

I missed my father. I hoped that he was okay. I hoped that he wasn't going too crazy knowing that I had been taken. At least he was aware that I was still alive and kicking – at least, that's what I had been able to pick up from the conversation between Tommy and the other one in the kitchen. It sounded as though they had a hard time working together, and I wondered if they'd really thought much about what they were going to do now that they had me. From everything that I had heard, it seemed like they were just rolling with the punches, trying to deal with everything as it happened, but that it wasn't turning out too well for them. At least, in Tommy's eyes.

And Amber – fuck, I missed Amber too. I knew that she must have been losing her mind with worry about me right now. I wished that I could see her, tell her that I was okay and that she had nothing to worry about – these men weren't going to do anything to hurt me, that much I was sure of. They needed me in one piece, and they knew that if they sent me back to my father hurting, there would be hell to pay.

Ironic, really, that they had to be more careful with me than my own fiancé did. I knew that Matt would have used this time to himself to terrorize me even further, to make sure I knew that he was the one in control. I had no doubt at all in my mind that he was going to somehow turn this all around and make it my fault that I had been kidnapped. I was dreading seeing him again, dreading how he was going to react. It was enough to make my stomach turn. I just had to keep trying to make the most of being in this fucked-up situation for as long as I could. I knew it wasn't normal to be grateful to the men who had kidnapped you, but right now, I felt as though they had saved me from something that nobody else had been able to.

Tommy had asked about my fiancé. As though he knew that there was something up there. I wished that I could tell him the truth about everything that that awful man had done to me, but I doubted that he would have believed me, even if I had. He wouldn't have believed that my father would let me be with someone so foul and so cruel; he wouldn't have believed that I had protected Matt all this time, made sure to keep his indiscretions and his cruelties to myself because I was scared of what might happen if I didn't. He would have thought I was insane.

Maybe I was. Maybe I should have gone to my next family gathering and made sure that everyone could see the bruises that he had left on me, the cruelty that he had written over my body. Then they wouldn't be able to deny it. They wouldn't have any choice but to see what he had done to me, see it and know that it had been them who had pushed me to be with a man as cruel and as foul as that...

But that was something I could deal with when I made it out of this mess. For the time being, I had to focus on making sure that I got through this with as little hurt as possible. And that meant befriending my captors.

Well, one, in particular. I got the feeling that Tommy was the softer-hearted out of the two of them – he seemed calmer, more grounded, more focused on what actually mattered. If I was going to get through to either of them, then I knew that it had to be him, and I intended to do everything that I could to make sure that happened.

He had allowed me to roam the house pretty much freely, and I had barely seen anyone else but him and me in that entire time; his brother was off in the city, by the sounds of it, dealing with everything that had come as a result of this scheme of theirs, and the security that they kept around must have been a little scattered across the property, making sure that nobody got in.

And that I didn't get out.

The thought of running was so far from my head in that instant that it seemed almost ridiculous to consider it. I didn't want to run. I wanted to stay, actually. Because this place was safe – at least, so far. I didn't know if it would stay that way, if something would shift that would cast me into a darker place, still trapped with those two men, but for now – for now, it was safer for me to remain.

I made my way out of my room, determined to go track down the other human that I knew was in here – the older brother seemed to have left once more, but Tommy remained. I wanted to get on his good side. If I was going to make it through all of this in one piece, then it started here, with him. He wouldn't be able to brush me off as nothing more than an irritation, the way that Matt always did. I had to get him to see me as a fully-formed human being, and I intended to start that right here, right now.

I headed down the stairs. The rest of the house was quiet, like it was holding its breath or something, and I liked the way that silence felt around me. It had been a long time since I had been able to enjoy peace like this.

Finally, I spotted some light spilling from a room that I hadn't been in before – the door was open a crack, and I took a deep breath and planted my hand on it so I could enter.

Inside, I was surprised to see Tommy surrounded by high bookcases, holding a book in his hand, reading quietly. Of all the things that I had expected to find, this was about the very bottom of all of my guesses. His eyes were focused on the page, his hand hovering over a drink in a glass on a small table next to him. It took him a moment to realize that I had even entered the room, and it wasn't until I cleared my throat that he looked up at me.

"Are you all right?" He sounded genuinely concerned, or at least, good enough at faking it that I couldn't tell the difference. I nodded.

"I'm okay," I replied. "Just – just didn't like being stuck up in my room all by myself, that's all."

I cast my gaze around the room. It seemed to be a library, well-stocked with books that I was instantly itching to get my fingers on.

"I didn't know you had a place like this here," I remarked, and I made my way to one of the bookcases, tracing my finger over the spines of some of the novels waiting there.

"My uncle filled this place with books," he explained. "And Jake – my brother—insisted that we at least keep them in one place. Hence why we have the library."

"I like it," I replied, and I smiled as I pulled out a familiar copy from the shelf in front of me. "Oh, this one – the Puzzle Piece trilogy, have you read it?"

"Finishing the last one right now," he replied, holding up the book that he was working on at that very moment. I felt my heart leap a little. I couldn't remember the last time that I'd had the chance to talk to anyone about books, since nobody in my circle seemed to care much about the damn things.

"It's such a good ending," I blurted out before I could stop myself. "I never would have seen it coming, but it makes so much sense when you think about it."

"Don't spoil it for me," he warned, lifting his finger up playfully to stop me in my tracks. "I haven't read nearly three whole huge books just to get the ending ruined right when I get to it."

"Sorry, sorry," I replied. "My lips are sealed."

I sank down on to the seat opposite him and looked over the copy of the book that they kept in their bookcases; it looked like a first edition and couldn't have been cheap.

"My mother's copy," he explained, as though he could sense the question that I had inside my head right now. "She always liked to have the best. I think a good chunk of this collection belongs to her, actually. Part of the reason I'm working my way through it."

"Oh, you trying to catch up with her back catalog?" I asked with interest. He smiled a little sadly.

"More trying to get a feel for all the things that she enjoyed," he explained. "She passed away when I was young. I like having these books of hers around. Makes me feel like I can still communicate with her, in some way or another."

"Oh, I'm so sorry," I murmured. "I – I lost my mom when I was young, too. It... changes you, I think."

"It does," he agreed. I was caught off guard by how honest I was being right now. There was a part of me that wanted to spring to my feet and pretend that none of this had happened at all and that I hadn't just told him something so honest, but truthfully, it didn't bother me. I wanted to talk to him. I wanted to get to know him. There was some...some draw to him, something that pulled me in when we were around each other.

Maybe because he was the first man in a hell of a long time that I didn't feel like I had to keep my wits about me with. Because I knew that if I was to say something wrong, then I didn't have to worry about him lifting his hand to me and threatening me with a beating.

Or maybe because of something as simple as the fact that he seemed to like books, too. Because nobody who liked literature, in my eyes, could be anything other than the right kind of person.

Chapter Twelve

Tommy

I WOKE THE NEXT MORNING, the book still in my hand, sprawled on the chair that I had been using in the library to relax the night before.

I peeled my head from the fabric and squinted up at the window opposite me – it was light out, and that meant that Jake was likely back by now.

I peered to the chair opposite me, half-expecting to still see Charlotte there opposite me, but she was gone. Even though not having eyes on her should have freaked me out, I wasn't worried.

The two of us had spent a good hour or two the night before talking—about books, mostly, about the stories that we loved the most. Seemed like we had the same taste in detective fiction, hard-boiled noir stuff that always turned out right in the end. Maybe some reflection of the world that the two of us were both caught up in.

Anyway, she had been good company, really good company, actually. So good that, by the time she retreated up to bed, I was relaxed enough to get some sleep. My mind had been racing ever since Jake had come back from the city and told me what he had been doing, but being around her made it all seem a little – a little easier, somehow. And I knew there was something to be said for that.

I marked the page that I had been at in my book, left it on the seat, and headed back through to the kitchen; I was starving, and I knew that Jake would have news. I wasn't even sure what his intentions were any longer, just that I needed to stay here and keep an eye on the girl, no matter what.

Not that she was making it hard for me to do that.

"Morning," I called to Jake as I entered the kitchen and found him lurking over the coffee machine, probably making himself something double-strength after he had been out all night. His head flashed around, and he narrowed his eyes at me.

"Where were you?" he demanded. "I went down to check your room and you weren't in there."

"I was in the library," I replied calmly. I didn't know what the hell he thought he was accusing me of, but I wasn't going to let it bother me. He was paranoid, that was the end of it. I didn't need to read anything into his accusations right now.

"How did it go in the city?" I asked. "What else did you find out?"

"Lou has people out looking for her, and us," he replied grimly. I cocked an eyebrow at him.

"Well, yeah," I replied. "I told you that would happen. It's not like they're just going to let you do anything you want because you've got her. If they can get out of paying that ransom, they're going to try. You get that, right?"

"Don't talk to me like I'm dumb," he replied, his eyes narrowing at me. "I know what I'm doing here."

"So you're just doing a really good impression of someone who doesn't know?" I asked. I knew that there was no good reason for me to rile him up, but shit, he had been pissing me off no end this week, since this whole mess had gone into action. I wasn't going to sit back and let him tell me how things were supposed to work, when I had told him that this was a bad idea in the first place.

"I have eyes on him," he shot back, deciding to ignore my snarky attitude. Probably for the best.

"Oh, yeah?" I asked. "And what's that for?"

"To make sure that I hit when he's desperate," he explained. He sounded downright pleased with himself, as though he had pulled off something amazing.

"And when you say hit…?"

"Make sure I give him the ransom information when he thinks he hasn't got a chance to get her back at all," he explained. "That's what I'm going to do. And I'm going to get every penny that I want from him…"

He trailed off, his eyes moving to something behind me. I turned just in time to see Charlotte slowly approaching the kitchen. She looked nervous.

"What the hell are you doing out of your room?" Jake demanded. She flinched as he raised his voice to her, and I wanted to tell him to shut the fuck up and calm down. We had no reason to be mean to her. The way she recoiled into herself was enough to tell me that someone else used that kind of language with her, too. Instantly, a wave of curiosity hit me – what else was she hiding?

"Jake, calm the fuck down," I told him. "You don't need to speak to her like that. We have everything under control."

"You better," he snarled at me, narrowing his eyes at her. She seemed frozen to the spot, like she wanted to vanish. I wished that I could pull her into my arms and tell her not to pay any attention to my brother, but I knew that he would have freaked out on both of us if I had tried anything like that.

"You need to keep a closer eye on her," he told me sharply. "We have her here for a reason. I don't want her just wandering around at random, okay? Keep her in her room, or—"

"She's not trying to get out," I told him. "She's not trying to leave. She just came downstairs. Now, stop talking to her like you've got a problem, all right?"

He didn't seem to have the energy in him to keep fighting with me. I locked eyes with Charlotte for a moment, and it seemed as though she was thanking me with the brief glance that we exchanged. I wished that

I could tell her that she had nothing to thank me for, that I would do anything I could to try and keep her safe. I wasn't sure what it was, but protectiveness had launched itself through me the moment that I had taken her into this house, and I knew it wasn't going to be so easy to get rid of it.

"I'm going back to the city," he told me. "And I'm going to stay there for a while. Keep an eye on things here."

"Sure," I muttered. I couldn't take my eyes off of her. There was something about the way she'd reacted to him that made me hurt for her, something that made me want to pull her into my arms and tell her that everything was going to be all right. I swore to myself that I would find out what it was that had her so tense.

"Good," he replied. "I need to stay in control here. You know that, don't you? You get that we have to make sure that Lou knows we're in charge—"

"I get it," I replied. I didn't want to hear another one of his speeches. I got that he wanted to seem like the big man around here, but I had already given over to his way of running things. As far as I was concerned, there was no point trying to fight it, because he had decided that it was going to be his way or no damn way at all.

"Good," he muttered, and he looked over at Charlotte again. Her eyes were fixed on the floor now, as though she was hoping that it might open beneath her and swallow her up.

"You make sure that nothing happens to her, all right?" he asked. "If we give her back with even a scratch on her, I doubt that her father will want to pay a cent."

"I'll do what I can," I replied. In truth, I didn't want anyone to lay a hand on her. I knew that she needed someone to take care of her, I knew that she was relying on me to be that for her. And I was going to do everything I could to make that happen. She needed a protector here, and I was going to make sure that was me.

"Nobody lays a finger on her, "he continued. "Nobody so much as touches her. I want her in pristine condition by the time that her father finally pays up."

"And how long is it going to be?" I asked him. "How long before you get the money you think you can get from him?"

"I don't think I can get anything," he corrected me. "I *know* that I can get that money out of him."

"Then when do you *know* that you'll get it?" I asked. He shook his head.

"I don't know yet," he admitted, and I almost laughed at how ridiculous it was – his overconfidence mixed with his inability to tell me what I needed to hear.

"You need to take some time to pull yourself together," I told him firmly. "Think a little. And then go back to the city. You can handle this all as it comes. Okay?"

"Fine," he muttered, though he sounded pissed about it. He had never liked being told what to do by me, though he was going to have to get used to it if he was going to be using me as security.

"I know it's going to get done on my terms," he continued as he brushed past me. I reached out to grab his arm, not willing to let him just walk away.

"Our terms," I corrected him. "It's going to be done on our terms. Isn't it?"

He stared at me for a moment, as though that thought hadn't crossed his mind. I knew that he wanted me to doubt myself right now, wanted me to second-guess everything. He saw this as his operation, and there was nothing that I could do to change that. I wanted to tell him to go to bed and let me handle it from here, but there was no way in fucking hell he would have let me take the lead now. Not when he had so much to prove.

"Sure," he replied, and he pulled his arm out of my grasp and stalked out of the kitchen. I knew that there was no point going after him, even though I wanted to chase him down and tell him that I wasn't going to stand for this fucking attitude of his – I didn't want him to talk to me like that, I didn't want him to think that he knew how to run this show, because he had shown a million times over that he didn't have a fucking clue.

But as Charlotte slowly raised her gaze to meet mine once more, I knew that there was no point going after him right now. Not when she was there. Not when it was so clear from the way that she looked at me that she needed me.

I jerked my head toward the kitchen, indicating for her to come join me.

"You want something to eat?" I asked. It took her a moment to respond, but when she did, she nodded.

"Yeah," she breathed. "Yeah, that would be great..."

Chapter Thirteen

Charlotte.

I DIDN'T KNOW HOW MUCH more of Jake I was going to be able to put up with before I flipped my shit and lost it for good.

I didn't know what it was about that guy. His attitude, the way he looked at me like I was nothing more than a small piece of dirt lodged into his shoe – whatever it was, it was enough to drive me insane, and I hated it. Hated the way he acted around me. He was the one who had stolen me away from my life, from my family, from my friends, and yet every time he looked at me, it was as though he could hardly contain his disdain. *Well, trust and believe, buddy, that the feeling is about as mutual as they come...*

Anyway. I knew that I needed to get in touch with someone back home. Amber, preferably – someone who I could tell that I was all right. That was the plan, what I was focused on for the time being, and I wasn't going to drop it until I saw it through.

Maybe it was just good to have something to stay focused on, because otherwise I might get too caught up in everything that had happened, everything that was still happening. I wasn't sure that I could handle the reality of my situation; that I had been kidnapped by these two men, and this place was going to be my prison for the foreseeable future.

I think the worst part of it, though, the part that made me feel the craziest, was that I felt safer here than I did in my own home. That was what I was trying not to think about, trying to push to the back of my head. I needed to forget that it had ever crossed my mind at all. I couldn't handle it, the reality of how dark my real life had become, that two men kidnapping me off the street would be than the man who I was supposed to spend the rest of my life with...

Anyway. The phone. I needed to get to it. I needed to make a call and get in touch with Amber.

Okay – it started with Tommy. He was the gentler of the two brothers. Jake was strutting around this place like he had everything to prove. He wasn't going to let me slip through his fingers so easily. Unless, of course, he was distracted with trying to get his brother back on his side – I wasn't sure what beef the two of them had, but it was clear that they had been at this for years and years, this power struggle between them.

Something about Jake just came off as false to me. I could tell that he wanted nothing more than to prove that he was powerful and in-control and that he knew how to run this show. But the darkness that you needed to mean it wasn't there with him.

I had seen that darkness, plenty of times, so up-close and personal that it couldn't have been mistaken for anything else. I knew what it looked like, what it felt like to be in the same room as that shit. I knew that you didn't need to spend your time making sure that everyone else could see it, that was for certain, but the way this guy went about things, it clearly hadn't clicked with him yet. Much as he might have wanted it to, I didn't believe that he was capable of doing much more than snapping at me in passing and hoping that it was going to be enough to keep me in my place.

The bad news for him was that it never would.

I still didn't know how they had managed to get as far as they had with all the tension between them. They seemed to disagree about everything, from what to do with me to how to spread butter on a damn dinner roll, and that was my key to figuring out a way through this. I was sure that I could exploit the gaps in their relationship to get what I needed. I just needed to be able to twist them in the right way. And Tommy was my way to do that.

I had tried to catch up with him a few times throughout the day, but every time I had gotten close to him, it seemed like Jake appeared out of nowhere to make sure that I couldn't do anything of the sort.

"What the hell are you doing out of your room?" he demanded as he appeared at the end of the hallway just as I came down the stairs.

"I'm hungry," I argued with him. Honestly, even though I knew that Jake wasn't going to get violent, it still spooked me, having a man speak to me like that. I had seen the bad end of that too many times not to be bothered by it. I had known, too well, what would happen if the man on the other end of that sharp tone of voice decided that he needed to teach me a lesson.

"Go back to your room," he ordered, pointing back up the stairs as though I was nothing more than an errant teenager. "I'll bring something up later."

I headed back up the stairs, wondering how the hell I was going to be able to get close to Tommy if his brother was going to be hovering around every corner. I needed to get him alone, and I wasn't going to be able to make that happen unless something seriously shifted – and soon.

Jake shoved some food through the door and then closed it tightly behind him, as though making double-sure that I wasn't going to come busting back out and wandering through the house again. I missed when it had been just Tommy and me, when he didn't seem to care about where I went or what I was doing provided I didn't make any trouble for him.

How could two boys who had presumably been raised in the same environment turn out so differently? It was a curious conundrum, and one that I found myself meditating on with all the time that I had up alone in my room right now. I didn't know what they had been through, if they had really grown up together or what, but there was something between them, something that seemed to shift and flex every time they were in the room together. Even though Jake wanted to be the one in control, he couldn't deny the fact that Tommy seemed to have that control without having to try at all. Interesting. And something that I could use to my advantage, if I knew how to twist it right...

Most of my time, I spent in my room. I knew that Jake would have locked me in there if he'd had his way, but luckily, it seemed like I had the other half of that squad advocating for me downstairs, because the door was never actually locked. I could hear them moving through the house, and I tried to train myself to recognize the sound of Tommy's footsteps so that I could oh-so-casually bump into him when I needed to speak to him.

I knew that they would have been able to tell that I was trying to manipulate him. And honestly, maybe I was – maybe this was all about getting my hands on that phone so that I could make a call back home and at least let them know that I was safe and that the person who was holding me here was about as incompetent as it was possible to be.

Person. Huh. Funny, how I thought of it like that – I thought of Jake as the only person forcibly keeping me here. Maybe because I felt as though Tommy was in this with me somehow. We both seemed to be bored with Jake, and Tommy seemed happy to spend time with me when he got the chance. When I had turned up in the library, he hadn't freaked out and told me to go back to my room – he had chatted with me, spoken to me like I was a real person.

And it had been a long time since a man had done that.

To most of the men I had met, even before Matt, I had been a means to an end. A way for them to get in the good graces of my father. Not as a person in my own right – no, heaven forbid they ever looked at me as that. They had to tiptoe around me for fear of pissing off one of the most powerful men in the city, and they seemed to all want me to know just how much they respected him.

But never how much they respected me. If they respected me at all.

And it had only gotten worse since I had been with Matt. They had been even more spooked, worried that they would disrespect both him and my father if they did the wrong thing, said something to me that might have been construed as anything other than careful, platonic conversation.

And I hated it. I hated being treated like I was nothing more than a way for people to get what they wanted. I knew that's what I had always been to Matt, even if he would claim to anyone who listened that he loved me, that he couldn't wait to spend the rest of his life with me.

I reached to touch the last bruise he had given me, the one on my jaw. It had almost started to fade now. I wouldn't have to cover it with makeup when I got back, which was a strange thought – I couldn't remember the last time I had just been able to walk out of the house without having to take the time to make sure that Matt's deeds were covered up. Couldn't remember the last time when I had been able to look myself in the mirror and not see the memories of him painted all over my skin, in bruises and scrapes and healing marks.

But here? Here, I didn't have to worry about that. And I was going to make the very most of that. I had no idea how long I was going to be stuck in this place, how long I was going to have to deal with Jake watching my every move and making sure that I knew that I couldn't do anything that would get him in trouble. But as long as it meant that I was far from Matt, I would take it.

For now. For now, I could live with this mess, because it kept me safe from the man I was supposed to marry. And I wasn't going to go fucking up my chance to be free from him.

Chapter Fourteen

Tommy

AS SOON AS JAKE'S CAR pulled out of the driveway, I let out a sigh of relief.

I didn't know why the fuck I had invited him to come stay an extra night. I knew that he needed to get some rest, but putting up with him all that time had been a downright nightmare.

There was a reason that Jake and I didn't live together, and it was because I knew he hated my guts. He would never have come out and admitted it, but he didn't have to – it was written all over his face, every time he looked at me.

But I had to push that to the back of my mind for now and make sure that it didn't get in the way of everything he had done, everything he still needed to do. I hated to rely on my brother for anything, but I knew that if I let him stay here with Charlotte, he would do something to hurt her. And I couldn't let that happen. Not just because I knew her father would have snuffed us both out in the blink of an eye if we had, but because she didn't deserve it.

I hovered outside her door for a moment, not sure if she would turn her back to me if I went in. I knew that Jake had been feeding her all this bullshit about needing to stay up in her room the whole time she was here, and I intended to undo that. I didn't care where she went in this house, as long as she stayed inside of it, and I knew that we were going to have more luck with her if we gave her some semblance of freedom than if we tried to clamp down on her doing anything.

I pushed the door open; she was inside, peering out of the window above her bed. She glanced up when she heard me come in.

"Oh, hello," she greeted me. She sounded hollower than before. She must have been missing her life back home, her family, her friends – I didn't blame her for sounding a little out of it. Especially after the way my brother had been acting lately.

"How are you?" I asked. It seemed a strange question to volunteer, given that we were the ones keeping her here, and that wasn't lost on her; she fixed her gaze on mine and raised her eyebrows.

"You really want to know the answer to that?"

"I'm sorry for the way my brother's been acting," I offered in response. She seemed to soften as soon as those words came out of my mouth. I knew that she must have been as irritated by him as I was, probably confused that the two of us had such different ways of going about things. We were supposed to be on the same team, but my brother had been acting like the two of us had never been in the same room before.

"What's up with him?" she asked. I snorted with amusement.

"That's the million-dollar question," I replied, and she managed a smile. I leaned up against the door, feeling somewhat more relaxed; something about being in her presence like this, the way she looked at me when I was alone with her, made me feel calm in a way that nothing else did.

"I mean, seriously, though," she remarked. "You must notice it too. It's so weird. He acts like he's trying to prove something to you..."

"I don't think it's me he's trying to prove something to," I explained. "It's our dad."

"Oh?" she replied, cocking her head to the side with interest. "What's he got to do with this?"

"Nothing, in a literal sense," I replied. "He died not too long ago. And Jake took over the...business. You know how it is. I think he just feels like he has to prove to everyone watching him at all times that he was the right choice to do that."

"And that's why he has to act like an asshole all the time?"

"That's why," I replied. She nodded. It seemed to be clicking inside of her head. I knew that I shouldn't have been feeding her so much information, but I didn't see any way that she could use this information against us; besides, it was clear that she had already started to notice something was up, no point in trying to hide it now.

"I get that," she remarked, shaking her head. "My sister, she – she can be the same with me sometimes."

"Oh?" I replied, prompting her to keep going. I wasn't sure what it was about her, but I needed to find out more. I needed to know what she was hiding from us – how she could be so confident half of the time, but occasionally snap back into this reticent, fearful version of herself that didn't seem to match with the other version.

"Yeah, Vanessa," she replied, shaking her head. "It's just – she's a little younger than me, and you know how girls can get at that age. She means well, but she's...insecure. Especially because I'm getting married. I think she thinks she needs to catch up with me or something. We used to be really close, but the more time that passes, the more I think she'd rather I wasn't in the picture at all."

"That sounds like a lot," I remarked, and she nodded.

"It is," she replied. "I think she'll grow out of it eventually, but she needs to settle into herself first. And I don't know how long it's going to take for her to do that, you know?"

"I know," I replied. She looked at me, smiled, shook her head.

"Sorry," she murmured. "I don't know why I'm telling you all of this. You don't need to hear about my sister..."

"It's okay," I assured her. "You can talk to me. If you want to, that is."

"I do," she replied, and she sounded as surprised as I was to hear those words come out of her mouth. I didn't expect her to be so honest with me. Didn't expect her to want to talk with me at all, but I was glad that she seemed willing to share these small details of her life with me. I liked the way she seemed to handle herself. Liked that she was willing to open up to me when the time came, when she was given the chance to.

"I wish I could get a little fresh air," she sighed, looking up to the window. I grimaced. I would have loved to take her out into the grounds, but I knew that it was far too much of a risk.

"I know, I know," she added on, with a slightly wan smile. "You can't do that. Because I might run away."

"You get it," I replied, and she nodded.

"I do," she agreed. "Just...thinking out loud, that's all."

She eyed me for a moment before she spoke again. I knew that there was a lot she wanted to say to me right now, a lot that she wanted to ask me. And I knew that I couldn't give her all the answers that she was looking for, much as I might have wanted to.

"You've been doing this all your life?" she asked, and I nodded.

"As long as I can remember, anyway," I replied. "Been in this business, same as Jake has."

"He's older?"

"Yeah, and that's why he acts the way he does," I replied, rolling my eyes. She chuckled as though she could feel that exact notion.

"I bet that's the same way that Van feels about me," she replied a little wistfully. I wondered how much she missed her family or if she was glad to be away from them, on some level. I didn't know, and I was sure that, if I asked, she would get defensive, tell me without a shadow of a doubt that she wanted to go home and get out of this place as soon as she could.

"Maybe," I murmured. She tucked her legs up and under herself, gazing at me as though there was so much she wanted to ask me but had no idea where to begin.

"I wish we were a little closer," she confessed. "Especially since we don't have our mother around anymore. I don't know, I always felt like I should have been there for her in that way – you know, looking out for her like our mom would have done if she had been alive. But..."

She trailed off, shook her head, and let out a long sigh.

"I guess it just wasn't meant to be," she finished up, her voice small and laced with sadness.

"You shouldn't have to step in and raise your sister," I protested. "Not when you could only have been a kid yourself, right?"

"Yeah, but logic doesn't really come into it when it comes to guilt," she replied a little sadly. "I just...I wonder if I had done things differently, if we might have had a different relationship by now, that's all. If she might have had a little more time for me. She might have actually liked me, who knows?"

"I'm sure she does," I replied. I knew that I was acting crazy – this woman didn't care one way or another if I thought her sister liked her or not. She was just passing the time by talking to me, maybe even trying to distract me from something else entirely, but I didn't care. I didn't want her being down on herself like that, especially when she had done nothing at all wrong.

"You don't have to try and sweet-talk me," she assured me, meeting my gaze steadily. "I know that you don't want to be here. This was all Jake's idea, wasn't it?"

She was sharp. I didn't know how much of our conversations she had overheard, but clearly, it was enough that she had wrapped her head around the ins and outs of our relationship. Normally, I would have been annoyed by someone getting to the heart of things just like that, but something about her knowing about it – I liked it. I liked the way that she talked to me, as though she already knew me inside and out.

Maybe because I wanted her to.

"You should get some rest," I told her. She laughed.

"Like I haven't been stuck inside here resting all day," she pointed out. I shrugged in acknowledgement.

"Yeah, but it doesn't look like you've actually been resting."

"You're one to talk," she protested. "You don't look like you've had a good night's sleep in weeks."

"Maybe I haven't," I replied, and she laughed again. I couldn't believe how lightly she was treating all of this, as though it was nothing more than a big-ass game to her. She truly was her father's daughter; I couldn't imagine anyone other than someone from their clan so calm in the face of what would have driven anyone else insane.

Or maybe I was just happy that she was smiling. And maybe I wanted to do anything that I could to ensure that the smile didn't get wiped off her face.

Chapter Fifteen

Charlotte

"CHARLOTTE?"

The sound of my name drew me out of my slumber, and I lifted my head to see who was talking to me. When I realized who it was, I couldn't keep the smile off of my face.

"Tommy?" I murmured, and I glanced around, wondering if it could really just be him. After everything that had happened, I felt as though I had to be due someone else now, someone like Jake, to come in and make everything worse.

"Come on," he told me, jerking his head towards the door. "Get dressed. Quickly. I have something to show you."

I pulled on my clothes without waiting for another word and hurried to join him at the door. I had no idea what this was about, but anything that could break up the monotony of the day would be welcome right now.

"What's going on?" I asked him as he guided me to the entrance hall. It was the closest I had gotten to leaving this place since I had arrived, and it almost felt dangerous being here, even with him.

"Keep your voice down," he told me softly, and he glanced around – and then pushed the door in front of me open and gestured for me to go outside.

I stared at him for a moment, and then at the sun-soaked grass just past the front path. Was he serious? He had told me yesterday that there was no way that we could do this, but now...

"What's going on?" I asked him, but he lifted a finger to his lips.

"We don't have long before someone notices that you're not in your room," he told me. "Come on. Let's go."

He grabbed my hand and pulled me out the front door – and even though it was cool with a morning freshness out there, I could feel myself warming from the inside out. What was going on? I didn't know, but there was no way that I was going to start arguing with it now. Not when it felt so right.

"Okay, what's happening?" I demanded again. Once he seemed sure that nobody was hanging around to catch us, he turned back to me.

"You said you wanted some fresh air," he pointed out. "I thought that I could do that for you."

"What happens if one of the other guards sees us?" I asked. He shrugged and grinned.

"Just going to have to hope that they don't," he replied, and he tugged me in close behind him. His touch was confident and controlled, as though he was telling me I had nothing to worry about. And I wanted to believe him – shit, I wanted to believe him so badly it was enough to make my head spin. I needed this to go the way I wanted it to; I needed this to turn out how I had hoped it would. I knew that it might not be easy, but any glimpse I got of the outside world right now was something that I would take as the gift that it was.

He guided me down a small path that was off the main line down to the house until the two of us arrived beside a lake at the edge of the property. It came up against the wall right beside where this place turned into the rest of the world, but I tried not to think about that. Instead, I focused on the drooping trees, the tendrils of their leaves so close to the water that they seemed to be reaching out to caress it.

"What is this place?" I asked him, and he grinned.

"Somewhere that nobody else bothers with," he replied. "So we don't have to worry about anyone finding us down here, as long as we get back to the house soon."

"What if we get caught?" I asked, and he shrugged.

"I can handle it," he replied, and I realized that my hand was still resting in his. I drew it back at once. I didn't want to even hint at the idea that I might be attracted to him.

Even though, with every passing moment, it was getting harder and harder to deny it.

I made my way down to the lake and reached down to skim my fingers over the clear blue water, watching as the ripples of my touch passed out over the water in front of me. I smiled. It felt like it had been such a long time since I had been outside. Not even just with being held here – even when I was back in the city, it wasn't as though I got much of a chance to be in nature, so trapped was I in the bright mess of buildings and cars and streets and roads.

"It's really beautiful," I murmured, and I turned to look back up at him. He stood there watching me, gazing down at me like he was thinking of saying the exact same thing.

"It really is," he agreed, and he came down by the water to join me. Something about his presence so close to me here made the hair on the back of my neck stand up. I did my best to ignore it, but there was only so much that I could do to pretend that it wasn't there.

"Do you think it's safe to swim in?" I wondered. He cocked an eyebrow at me.

"Only one way to find out," he remarked, and he pulled off his shirt and slipped beneath the water before I could say another word. I burst out laughing as he broke the surface again, teeth chattering from the cold.

"Is it that bad?" I asked, and he shrugged, as though he was trying to play it cool.

"Only one way for you to find out," he shot back, and my lips parted into a smile. I liked the way he talked to me, as though he knew that he had me right where he wanted me. I couldn't remember the last time someone had made me feel that way, and I didn't want to let it go.

"You coming in?" he asked. I glanced around. There was nobody out here but us, and I didn't know how long it would be before he could sneak me out of the house again. Why not? I might as well make the most of it...

I dived beneath the water before I could talk myself out of it, and I had to stifle a shriek at how cold it was. It caught me off-guard, made my whole body seize up for a moment, but I managed to keep it off my face, play it cool.

"So, what do you think?" he asked. "Good for swimming?"

"I don't know about that," I replied as I splashed this way and that. Honestly, I didn't care much about the cold right now – all that mattered to me was that I was free in this place, that I didn't have to worry about someone appearing to tell me to get the hell out of that water and stop acting the fool. I could do what I wanted. And I intended to prove to myself that this was the best way that I could live my life.

"Yeah, agreed," he replied with a chuckle. He reached out to brush a strand of hair off my face, and without thinking, I flinched away from him. He frowned.

"Sorry," he murmured. "I didn't mean to scare you."

"You didn't," I replied. As if he ever could – honestly, I just wanted to fall into his arms and let him hold me, let him close to me in a way that nobody had ever been before in my life. But I was still so fucked up from everything that Matt had done to me, I didn't know where to start.

"Did someone hurt you?" he asked me. I took a deep breath. I didn't know what to tell him. This was a man who had snatched me off the street, a man who had apparently done far worse to me than so many of the people in my life, and yet, he seemed to care about me more than any of them did. And I wasn't sure how to feel about that.

"It...it doesn't matter," I replied. I wanted to forget about it, but I knew that he wasn't going to let it slide through his fingers just like that.

"Yes, it does," he replied firmly, and he reached out to cup my face in his hand, to look into my eyes properly. I didn't flinch this time. I knew that I didn't have to. I just wanted to lean into him, let him touch me in a way that nobody had ever touched me before. I could feel something burning inside of me, something alight with excitement every time he laid hands on me, and I was certain that he could make it out, too.

"Was it your father?" he asked. I shook my head immediately.

"He would never hurt me," I replied, and I meant it. My father was many things, but he loved Van and me fiercely. He would never have hurt us.

"Then who?" Tommy asked. "Who would do that to you?"

His voice cracked as he said it, as though he was genuinely wondering what the hell was going on back in my real life. And shit, there was a part of me that wanted to tell him all the secrets that I had been keeping inside of me all this time.

But I knew I couldn't do that. Because if I started talking, I might never be able to stop, and if I couldn't stop, then I didn't know how the hell I was going to be able to kiss him right now.

I moved a little closer, not taking my eyes from him. Damn, he was so beautiful—that dark hair, those dark eyes, searching me, looking for an answer, for something that would tell him what was going on inside my head. I wanted to lean myself into him and let him hold me, let him pull me close and tell me that everything was going to be okay and that he would be able to protect me from everything that was going to come piling down on our heads when they found me again.

But for now, all I could see was him, this man who cared enough about me to want to know what pain I had suffered. And shit, it had been so long since anyone had actually given a damn that I had almost forgotten what it felt like.

His fingers traced my face, and this time, I didn't pull away. I didn't want to. I wanted him to touch me, to hold me, to show me all the ways that he was willing to protect me. But I knew that I had to be the one to make the first move. He wouldn't push me, he wouldn't do anything that he didn't think I was totally ready for.

And so I closed my eyes, leaned forward, and pressed my lips against his.

Under the cool embrace of the water, it was almost as though we were hidden from the rest of the world – almost as though the two of us were here alone, removed from anything that might have existed outside of the confines of this space. He didn't kiss back for a split second, as though he was making sure that this was really happening, but as soon as it clicked for him that it was, his tongue parted my lips, and his hands came to my waist, and he pulled me against him like I was the only thing in the world that he cared about.

His touch was electric, fiery, coursing through me in a way that nothing else had before. Nobody had ever wanted me the way that he did, so willing to put everything that he had worked for at risk if it meant that he could have me in that moment. He tilted his head, his hand coming to the back of my neck so that he could pull me close to him, and he kissed me like he had been starving for me for as long as he could remember. Maybe he had. Maybe, like me, it had been from the very first moment that he had laid eyes on me, and he didn't want to forget the intensity of that desire for a second.

He pulled me back towards the earth again, and the two of us scrambled from the water and pulled off the rest of our sopping-wet clothes under the shield of the trees around us; his hands moved over my body, guiding off what I had been wearing, and his lips traced over every fresh inch of skin that I exposed in the process. It was like he was trying to consume me, in the best way possible, like he was trying to take me in, make me his. I liked it. I wanted to sink against his body and have him hold me so close that nothing else was ever able to get near to me. We were meant for one another, and I could feel that now, deep down in my soul – it might not have been how normal people came to find one another, but with him, right now, I knew it was true.

He kissed me again, harder this time, as he pushed me to the soft earth below us. His touch was more powerful this time, guiding me to something more intense, and I knew that I had to feel him inside of me. I wanted him. I lusted for him. I could feel his hardness nestled against the inside of my thigh, and I knew it would only take the slightest shift of my hips to guide him inside of me for the first time. And hell, I wanted it so badly I couldn't think straight, couldn't think of anything but the power of the way he touched me – I knew that I was engaged to someone else, and if any of this was exposed, I would be ruined in a way that I had never thought possible before.

But when he brushed his lips across my ear, his breath on my skin, and whispered those words to me – *Can I fuck you?* – there was only one word that I could find in answer to that.

"Yes," I breathed back at once. And, with that, he took himself into his hand, and moved inside me for the first time.

I had to bury my head into his shoulder to keep from letting out a helpless little moan of pleasure – I knew that I had to control myself. If we were caught together, people would assume things that I wouldn't be able to disprove, and I didn't want anything getting in the way of this, of how good it felt. I grasped his shoulders, feeling the strength of his muscles underneath his skin, and I wanted to pull him into me. Not just like this, but for good, forever, I wanted to bond with him in a way that I had never bonded with anyone before.

He wrapped his arms around me and shifted so that he was driving into me even deeper, filling me in long, hard strokes that made my entire body tremor with excitement. I didn't know how he could do it, how he could make me feel this good, but I didn't care. All that mattered right now was giving myself over to the sensation of it, letting it rush through me, the way I had needed it to from the start. The way I had needed him to.

We seemed to fit together as though we had been made for each other. His mouth moved to mine again, and he kissed me hard as he flexed his hips against mine, moved in slow circles inside of me, taking his time, as though he was really enjoying every moment of this thing that we had together right now. I loved the way he felt. I skimmed my fingers down his bare back, tracing my nails over his skin, wishing that I could scratch them deep and leave marks but knowing that I needed to play it cooler. If I left anything that could connect me to him, that could prove that this had really happened, I knew that we would both be in trouble.

Though it was hard to care about that when he felt so fucking good moving inside of me.

I couldn't contain myself, couldn't control myself – I wanted more, I wanted everything that he could give me and then some. I wanted to give myself over to this man utterly and completely, this man who had seen something like suffering in me and instead of ignoring it had drawn me in close to him, let me find some safety when I felt like I hadn't seen anything like it in a million years.

"You feel perfect," he murmured against my ear, his lips on my skin so that I could feel the words as much as I could hear them. I arched my back, telling him that I needed him deeper, deeper, telling him that I needed everything he was willing to give me right now.

And, sure enough, it didn't take long until the burning heat inside of me had started to swell and grow beyond the point that I could control it any longer. My breath was tearing out of me, the cold drips of water running down my skin feeling as though they might just boil to life on the spot with the heat that we were creating. The burning in my belly was growing with every thrust he made inside of me, each and every movement he filled me with, and I buried my head into his shoulder to hold back the inevitable cry when I-

I managed to hold it in. But the orgasm still ripped through me, my entire lower body tensing up for a moment before I could stop it, the thrill of that release enough to give me everything that I had been waiting for. My entire system was built for this, around him, around the way that he fucked me, and he must have known it. A few moments later, I felt his cock twitch inside of me, his warm seed flooding into me, deepening our bond even further. I knew that this was risky, in all the ways that it was possible to be risky, but I didn't give a damn about that. I just wanted to feel him, every part of him that he would let me feel.

He continued to move inside of me, slower this time, moving carefully, as though worried that he would break me if he went too hard and too fast. I kissed his shoulder and neck, feeling the roughness of his stubble against my lips and craving more.

But as he kissed me back, I knew that the two of us were going to have to play it careful if we were going to get away with what we had just done. If we got caught, everything would be ruined. And there was no way in hell I was willing to give up the intensity of the chemistry between us right now.

No matter what.

Chapter Sixteen

Tommy

I LEANED ON THE WALL just outside her door, wondering when I was going to let myself in.

I had to see her again. I wasn't willing to wait another moment to lay eyes on the woman that I hadn't been able to get out of my head this entire time.

It wasn't like I had never been with a woman before. I'd had plenty, back in the city, though none of them had managed to convince me they were worth keeping around for more than a night. Maybe I just hadn't wanted to give them the chance – that seemed more likely. I tried to push that to the back of my head. I didn't want to think about anyone else.

The sex had been incredible. But it was more than that. The connection that we shared was electric, something that I couldn't remember having with anyone before in my entire life. I loved the way she talked, the way she tilted her head to the side as she listened to me, the way that she touch me as though she could hardly believe that I was right there with her. She was the kind of girl a guy could get addicted to, way too easily.

And I think she knew that, too.

I was certain that we couldn't do what we had done again. Not out in the grounds, anyway. If anyone caught us hooking up, then there would be hell to pay. Jake would turn on both of us, and me, especially. He would never forgive me, and the last thing I wanted to deal with right now was the consequences of him turning on me.

But he was in the city for the time being, and that meant that I had her all to myself. There was no way that I was going to pass up an opportunity like that. I wanted to make the most of the time that I had with her before the real world came back in to bite at our heels, and I knew that the two of us didn't have long.

I knocked on the door and pushed it open before I could talk myself out of it. She was lying in the bed, on top of the covers, with the book that she had picked out from the library the day before when I had been bringing her back to the house. She had asked for a chance to poke around in the books, and honestly, she could have asked me for anything that she wanted in that moment, and I wouldn't have been able to say no. I was so enamored with her, the way she moved, the way she talked, the way she acted, and I didn't want anything to get in the way of that.

She lifted her head and smiled when she saw it was me, sitting upright and gesturing for me to come in. I headed over to join her, planting myself down on the edge of the bed, wanting nothing more than to slip beneath the covers with her and pretend that the rest of the world didn't exist for a little while.

"How are you?" I asked. The words seemed too tiny to sum up everything that was going through my head, but I had to start somewhere.

"I'm fine," she replied. I knew that she couldn't be telling the truth, but I wanted to hear everything that I could from her right now. I wanted to prove to her that I could be everything that she needed me to be, no matter what. I wanted to show that I was able to help her the way that she needed to be helped, even though I was the one keeping her here against her will.

I wished that I had the nerve to bring that up, but I didn't even know where to start. I wanted to tell her that I had enjoyed everything that we had done the night before, but I wasn't sure that she would have believed me. Maybe she thought I was taking advantage of her, using her vulnerable position to get what I wanted out of her...

Or maybe I needed to stop overthinking everything and just fucking ask what was going on inside her head right now.

"Did you sleep well?" I asked. She nodded and smiled.

"Better than I have any other night since I got here," she replied, and she fluttered her lashes at me with a playful flirtation. "Guess something must have tired me out, huh?"

"Guess it must have," I agreed. I couldn't help but grin back. Even now, the chemistry between us was burning-hot, so intense that I was sure she could feel it, too. I had told the guards to stick to patrolling the border of the property, and I knew that we weren't going to be interrupted. I could have just slipped under those covers with her, forgotten about everything else I had to do today, pretended that none of it mattered at all...

"It was...it was really good," she blurted out, and I laughed. It was clear that she wasn't used to talking like this, but I appreciated that she was willing to go out of her way to make sure that I knew how much she loved it. It would have been all too easy to spin it as something that she had only done because she didn't want to get on my bad side, but I knew that what we'd shared was real.

"I know," I agreed, and I slid my hand out over hers, our skin touching for just the briefest moment – fuck, even that was enough to make my whole chest light up. Just being near her made the hair on the back of my neck stand up, and I knew that I would have to work double-time to keep from showing that to anyone else by the time my brother came back.

"I was wondering," she murmured as she traced her fingers along the back of my hand and up my wrist. "Could I make a call?"

I didn't reply. She already knew what the answer to that question would be. I couldn't let her speak to anyone, no matter how much she might have wanted to. It wasn't safe. I knew it wasn't safe. And I was sure that some part of her recognized that as well.

"I can block the number," she offered, as though that would make a difference. "I just want to speak to my best friend, you know, let her know that I'm okay and that I'm not hurt or anything. Not for long, but..."

She trailed off, sensing the answer before it even came. She sighed.

"I guess that's a no?"

"I wish I could," I replied, and I meant it. I knew that, in the grand scheme of things, it wouldn't matter if she spoke with her best friend from a blocked number for just long enough to tell her that she was doing okay. But I couldn't hide a call being made, and if Jake got back and caught wind of it, he would lose his fucking shit. And that was the very bottom of the list of things that I wanted to handle right now.

"I know," she replied, and she sank back on to the bed as though she was ready to go back to sleep for the day. I wanted to lie down with her, but I didn't think that she would have wanted me there after I had just told her no on the one thing that she had wanted.

"If Jake finds out, he'll—" I began, but she lifted her hand to stop me in my tracks.

"I get it, it's okay," she assured me. "I know that I'm still...I know that you have me here. You get to decide how all of this goes."

I didn't reply. I didn't want to think of this like that. In truth, I really didn't see it that way – I knew that she had every right to, given everything that she had been through, but this was still Jake's idea in my head. An idea that I had been stuck with going through with because I couldn't come up with any better answers to the questions that he had tried to pose to me.

And now I was here, with her, and I was starting to feel something real – starting to sense something coming to life between us, something that I couldn't deny even if I wanted to. And I didn't know how I could convince her that she had nothing to fear from me, that she had nothing to worry about. That I would have given her everything that she wanted if it meant that I could see her face light up the way I wanted it to right now.

She would never have believed I was telling the truth. I didn't blame her. But that meant I was going to have to work double-time to prove to her that I really meant it when I said that I cared about her. For more than she could give us as the victim of Jake's twisted little scheme.

Chapter Seventeen

Charlotte

I WANDERED DOWN TO the library, glancing around as I did so to make sure that Jake wasn't back. I knew that he would lose it if he saw me out of my room, and frankly, I didn't feel much like dealing with his shit right now. I knew that he was probably being sensible, not letting me do anything I wanted or go anywhere that I pleased, but to be quite honest, I was getting seriously tired of having to play by his rules.

Especially when he wasn't even here to enforce them. And especially when I could tell that Tommy didn't want anything to do with them.

I had asked him about the phone the morning before, and he had told me that he couldn't do anything for me – I knew that it was a long shot, but I had been praying that I could actually talk to someone else, let them know what was going on and get through to them in a way that would soothe some of the worries I was sure they were having right now. Amber, especially – I knew that my father would be too caught up in the anger of someone having taken me in the first place to actually want to hear my voice, but Amber would actually care. She would want to know that I was okay, and I wished that I could get through to her and tell her that she had nothing to worry about.

Not as long as Tommy was here with me, at least.

I knew that he cared for me. I could see it in the way he looked at me – in the way he was careful not to push too hard for something that I couldn't handle. He was well aware of the power dynamic between us, that he was the one in charge, and so, he was sure not to press for more than I wanted. I had to be the one to come to him, and I knew that.

I knew that.

Ugh. I just wanted to speak to someone else. I would have been happy with just Tommy, but I needed the people back in my real life, the people who were worried about me, to know that I was all right. They had probably decided that I was already gone, lost to them for good, and I was far from it. I was still here, still alive and kicking, maybe more alive than I had been in a long time.

Because I didn't have to worry about Matt here. Not him hurting me, not me doing or saying the wrong thing and having him turn it around on me a moment later. Tommy was the polar opposite of him in every way, and it scared me, in some ways, to think about leaving him after everything that had happened. Because I was certain that Matt would be able to tell that something had happened between us – and even though it was fine for him to go off and cheat on me with every woman that he could find to open their legs for him, I got the feeling that he wouldn't extend the same kind of courtesy to me.

I returned the book that I had taken from there the day before and started browsing everything else that they had. There was so much I didn't know where to start. I wished that Tommy was here with me right now; he always had a good recommendation for me, something that I never would have thought to pick out for myself but that fit my tastes perfectly.

"Hi."

I whirled around, my heart leaping up into my chest, not sure if I should be scared or glad – but when I saw it was Tommy standing there in the doorway, I couldn't keep the smile off my face.

"Hey," I greeted him, my whole heart leaping upwards in my chest. Just being in the same room as him made everything better, and I wished that I could come a little closer and snuggle against him. But there was a serious expression on his face that made me stop in my tracks.

"What is it?" I asked him, and he pulled something out from his pocket and held it out to me. In the dim light of the library, it took me a moment to work out what it was – but then he clicked a button and it lit up, and I realized that he was offering me a phone. My eyes widened, and I gasped.

"Holy shit, Tommy!" I exclaimed, and I grabbed it from him at once. "Is this...?"

"It's a burner," he told me, pulling the door shut behind us as though making sure that nobody was going to hear the conversation. "And you can make a call on it. Just one call, okay? The number and location is blocked, so they can't get back in touch with you, and I'm going to be in the room the entire time—"

"I get it," I breathed, and I stared down at it, feeling tears prick the backs of my eyes. I couldn't remember the last time that someone had done something so sweet for me. I took a deep breath, gathering myself. I knew just who I was going to call, just what I was going to say.

"Can you give me a minute?" I asked him, and he nodded, taking a step back so that I could have the privacy I needed. He didn't leave the room, but I was fine with that. It wasn't like much of what I told the person on the other end of this call was going to be true, anyway.

I dialed the number that had been burned into my brain ever since Amber had gotten her new phone and had spent the next three days getting me to recite it so that I would always be able to get in touch with her if I needed to. And, sure enough, a few seconds later, the call was answered, and I heard my best friend at the other end of the line.

"Hello?"

"Hey, Amber," I greeted her, trying to keep some urgency to my voice, to make it sound as though I was being watched or something.

"Oh shit, Char?" She gasped. "Is that you?"

"It's me," I replied. "I don't have long—"

"Are you okay?" she demanded. "Where are you?"

"I'm fine," I replied at once, trying to avoid the other question.

"They're not hurting you, are they?" she asked. "Who took you? Where are you—"

"I don't know the names of the people who took me," I lied, trying to ignore the start of guilt in my chest at lying to my best friend. I knew that she just wanted to get me out of this mess in one piece, but she didn't know what she was going to be sending me back to if she did, and I didn't want to go so soon.

"But I'm okay, they're not hurting me, and if they haven't started by now, they're not going to," I assured her. "I just – I'm okay. I'm all right."

"How can you be?" she demanded. "You were kidnapped. Oh my... Char, I need to tell everyone that I heard from you—"

"No, no, don't tell anyone," I pleaded with her. "Just...keep this to yourself, okay? I don't want you getting dragged into this, and if my father finds out that you spoke to me, that's just what's going to happen."

"I can't keep this from them, Char. They're all looking for you—"

"Please," I replied, and I meant it. I didn't want anyone else hearing about this. I didn't want anyone else knowing that I had so much as whispered a word to her. She would get dragged down into this and she didn't deserve that, not really, not here, not now.

"Fine," she sighed. "But your father is looking for you, you know. I think he's got the whole city on high alert to find you."

"I thought he would," I agreed. "But just promise me you're not going to say anything to him, okay? Or anyone. I just wanted to tell you that I was okay."

"You have my word," she promised. "Can I call you back on this number? Or..."

"No, don't," I replied at once. "I just managed to get this phone off one of them, if they get a call from you, they'll know that I've been in touch with people outside and I won't be able to hide it."

"Of course, of course," she muttered. "Just...do everything you can to get your hands on another phone, okay? I want to talk to you again. I want to know that you're okay."

"I will," I replied. "I have – I have to go now, Amber, I'm sorry. But please, don't worry about me. I'm going to be just fine."

"You better," she replied, and I managed to laugh, even though it hurt a little not to be able to see her laughing with me.

"I have to go," I told her again, and she said goodbye quickly before I hung up. I hesitated for a moment, and then handed the phone back to Tommy. He took it from me, dropped it to the ground, and brought his boot down on it hard, over and over, until it was shattered into a pile of twisted pieces.

"Thank you," I murmured to him, and I meant it. He looked back at me. He knew that he had risked something huge in doing what he had done, but I got the feeling that he didn't really mind.

"It means so much to me," I told him, and I reached out to take his hand, the one that wasn't holding on to the scraps of the phone that he had scooped up from the floor. He brushed my hair back from my face, and this time, I didn't find myself flinching away from his touch. I wanted him to touch me. And it had been a long time since I had been able to say that about anyone.

He leaned down to kiss me, and as soon as our lips touched, I felt myself melting against him. I knew that I was never going to be able to get over this man, the small kindnesses that he had showed me, even when he had no reason to. He could have landed himself in no end of trouble just for a small gesture like this, but he was still willing to go through with it, because he knew it was what I needed.

"I know," he murmured back, and he kissed my cheek again and turned to stride out of the library, presumably to get rid of the pieces of the phone that he was still holding on to. I lifted my fingers to my lips and touched the spot where his mouth had been, as though I was trying to bring back the feeling.

I knew that I was falling for him. More than I should ever have let myself fall for someone who had kidnapped me. But there was no denying the intensity of our feelings towards each other, or the way that his kiss made me feel.

Chapter Eighteen

Tommy

SITTING WITH MY BACK to the shower, giving her the privacy to get herself together, it took everything that I had in me not to turn around and face her, watch her gloriously naked body underneath the water, the way she moved as it caressed her skin.

This had become our schedule every day since Jake had left. She would take a shower first thing in the morning, and I would sit there in the doorway, my back to her, ostensibly so that I could keep an eye on her – but really, I knew it had everything to do with just wanting to be close to her.

I knew that I had been pushing my luck with the phone call yesterday, but I couldn't just turn her down after everything that she had been through. She needed to talk to someone, and there was no way I was going to deny her that.

I had taken the broken pieces of the phone out of the library and straight down to the lake to dispose of them – I had watched as they bobbed on the surface for a little while and then vanished underneath. I wasn't even sure that Jake knew this place existed, and I was sure that he wouldn't think to come down here looking for the remnants of what I had tried to hide from him.

At least, that's what I hoped.

I knew that I would be in danger if he found out what I had done for that girl. That she would be, too. I didn't want her to have to pay for what I had done, but I knew that Jake would turn it on her and make sure that she suffered for the small bit of kindness that I had shown her.

I hadn't heard from my brother in a while now, and I wouldn't have been surprised if he was just strutting about the city right now, making sure that everyone knew what a big fucking man he was for having stolen away the daughter of one of the most powerful people in the city. He would be dining out on this for a long time to come, I knew that much – I knew him well enough to understand that he was going to do everything that he could to prove that this made him something better than he actually was, even though I could see through it, see through the lies that he had formed around himself.

I had overheard the conversation that she'd had with her friend on the phone the day before, and I hadn't been able to stop thinking about it since. Not because I believed there was some hidden meaning to it or anything, that she had been secretly signaling to her without my knowledge, but because she hadn't chosen to call up her fiancé. She had been speaking to a woman, and I knew that I would have heard about it by now if the daughter of Lou Saint Clare was involved with a chick – and I guessed that she wouldn't have been able to fake the intensity of our chemistry if she had really been stuck on girls, anyway.

By the time that she emerged from the shower – soft and damp, her skin so deliciously tempting that I had to fight the urge to just reach out and touch her – she was humming to herself, apparently in a better mood than she had been before. I wondered what was going through her head, how much she had thought about the call that she had made the night before.

"You okay?" she asked me as she brushed past me and into the bedroom to get dressed. I rose to my feet and nodded.

"I'm fine," I replied. "Can I ask you something?"

She glanced over her shoulder at me and cocked an eyebrow, then nodded.

"Yeah, of course you can," she agreed. "What's up?"

"Why didn't you call your fiancé yesterday?"

As soon as the words were out of my mouth, she seemed to still for a moment. Like I had said something that she didn't know the answer to. She got the clothes out of the dresser – I had picked some up for her in my last trip to the nearby town, so that she would have something fresh to wear – and started to dress slowly. She seemed in no rush to cover herself up, and I was glad that she felt so comfortable in front that she didn't have to worry about hide her body from me.

"I didn't want to talk to him," she replied. But she didn't look at me as she said it. Like she was trying to hide something from me.

"Why not?" I wondered aloud. "Don't you want him to know that you're okay?"

She fell silent again. Every word that she spoke now, it was as though she was picking it carefully. When she replied to me at last, it was as though she was trying to hold something back, trying to make sure that I didn't find out anything more than she wanted me to.

"It's complicated," she replied.

"How?" I pressed her. She shook her head. I needed to know what was going on with her – I needed to know why she seemed so spooked by me bringing him up. Something was going on under her skin right now. Something that she didn't want to reveal to me.

But something that I was determined to get out of her, one way or the other.

"I didn't want to speak to him," she replied with a shrug. "That's all."

"Won't he be worried about you?" I asked her. She shook her head and snorted, as though the thought of it was silly.

"What's going on with that guy?" I asked her. She fell silent. I knew that there was something that she was hiding from me, something that she didn't want to say out loud. But I needed to know what was in her head right now. I needed to know what was happening with her fiancé that seemed to have her so happy to be away from him.

"Nothing," she replied. But her eyes slid away from mine as she spoke, and it was clear that she wasn't telling the truth.

"Please, Charlotte," I murmured, and I reached out for her hand. She let me take it, looked down at my fingers resting against her skin, and sighed.

And then, finally, she looked up and into my eyes. And gave me the answer that I had been looking for.

"Are you sure you can handle this?" she asked, chewing her lip. I nodded. I could take anything, as long as it was the truth. She took a deep breath, and then gazed into my eyes and began to speak.

And the shit that came out of her mouth – it was the last thing that I had expected to hear about this fiancé of hers. I couldn't believe what I was hearing. This man who was supposed to be marrying her in just a few months' time was nothing more than an abusive piece of shit, subjecting her to a campaign of vile terror that had left her too scared to tell anyone.

She spoke quickly and quietly, as though she was worried that someone might overhear us at any moment, and I held her hand tight the entire time. I wanted her to know that I was right there beside her and that I wasn't going anywhere, and that I didn't think anything different of her now that I knew what she had been through. She seemed almost ashamed of what she had put up with from that man, but it wasn't her who should have been ashamed. It was him, for hurting a girl as sweet and as gentle as she was, for taking out his anger on someone he knew would never be able to stand up to him. It was enough to make me sick, and it took everything in me not to get to my feet, storm out, and go find this guy once and for all to kick his ass.

When she was done, I got to my feet. I needed to control myself. I didn't want to scare her – I didn't want her to think that she had been wrong to tell me that story, after all the strength that it had taken for her to come out with it. She deserved to be taken care of. She deserved a man who would protect her.

She watched me from the bed, as I paced back and forth in the room. I wanted nothing more than to pull her into my arms and tell her that everything was going to be all right, but I doubted that she was going to believe me. Not after everything that she had told me. Not after all that she had been through.

"Are you okay?" she asked me finally, her voice timid. I hated that she thought she had any reason to fear me. That bastard of a fiancé of hers had instilled this in her, this sureness that this was what she needed to do around men. If I ever got my hands on him – if I ever got close to him-

I gathered myself. I needed to show her that I was different than the man who had hurt her so badly in the past. I needed to prove to her that she had nothing to fear from me, and I intended to make sure that I never scared her, never gave her reason to fear me, never gave her reason to think that I would lash out in the way that he had.

Much as I wanted to slam my fist into the wall, I knew that it would only scare her. And the last thing I wanted right now was to give her any reason to fear me.

Her eyes were locked on mine, searching for some kind of explanation. I wanted to tell her everything that she needed to hear right now, but honestly, all I could focus on was the white-hot rage burning through my skin and my brain so that I could barely think.

"I need a minute," I told her, and with that, I turned and walked out of the room. I knew that she would be left wondering if she had done or said something that was too much for me to handle, but she hadn't. I just wanted some time to myself so that I could work out how much I wanted to say to her about what she had been through – and so I could figure out just how I was going to take that foul fiancé of hers down for good. I knew that it was going to be hard, but there was no way I could leave him to walk the earth knowing what he had done to her. The world would be a better place without a man like that in it.

And I intended to do the earth the favor of wiping him off the face of it for good.

Chapter Nineteen

Charlotte

CURLED UP IN THE BED and listening for the sound of his footsteps outside the door, I wondered if I had done the right thing in telling him the truth.

He had asked, and I had told him. I still couldn't believe that I had spilled it to him that easily, not after everything that I had been through. After I had spent so long keeping that secret to myself, it was almost second nature to laugh off any concerns and assure everyone that I was doing just fine.

It still sent a jolt through my system to think that I had been able to come clean about all of it to a man like that. I had been so practiced in lying, deflecting, pretending that I didn't know anything about why they might have been coming to me with these worries, that I had almost convinced myself that it was true.

But now I was being honest. And I could say that everything that Matt had done to me had scarred me deeper than anything else in my life. And that if I had to go back to him, I didn't know how I was going to cope.

I was pretty sure that I had scared Tommy off, dropping everything on him like that. I knew that it must have been a lot for him to take in. He just wanted to get to the bottom of all of it and I had hit him with something that was so much darker than anything he could have anticipated. Not exactly fair, was it? But then, I had to tell him the truth – I didn't want to keep Matt's secrets any longer.

Not when I had finally met a man who made me feel the way that I was sure I was supposed to feel.

Was this Stockholm syndrome or something? Me thinking that the people who had kidnapped me actually cared about me? No, it couldn't have been that, because the other one, his brother, still irritated me as much as he ever did. But Tommy – Tommy was something else. When I thought about him, it was as though I could feel something blooming inside my chest, something so sweet and so fresh and so new that I almost didn't want to even look at it for fear that it might fall to pieces before it had a chance to brighten into its final form.

He had left me alone after our conversation, and I supposed that it was for the best, really – I needed some space to myself to work out everything that had just happened, how the hell I actually felt about all of it. I knew that I needed to be careful, play it safe, not spill too much to him, but I wanted to tell him everything. It was such a relief, such a catharsis, and I didn't want it to end...

Anyway. I wasn't going to sit around in bed and wait for him to turn up. I was going to go find him, talk to him about everything that had happened, and then maybe we could cut to the chase and get over this. I climbed out of bed, headed out into the hallway, and started padding downstairs towards the kitchen. I felt like I needed something to eat, something to replenish my stores after everything that I had been through and everything that I had just spilled.

"How long till you're back?"

I heard his voice on the other end of a phone line, and I froze halfway down the stairs. He must have been talking to his brother. I didn't move a muscle – I wanted to hear everything that they were saying. I didn't know if, perhaps Tommy had been trying to get something more out of me to use against my family or my father, but now would be the chance to find out. I planted myself down on a step and shifted as close to the edge as I dared without letting him see me.

"Yeah, yeah," he remarked, as though brushing off what Jake was saying to him. "Listen. There's something I need to ask you. About the fiancé, Matthew. Have you got eyes on him as well?"

I felt my shoulders tense to my ears as soon as I heard Tommy say his name. He spat it, like it was poison he was trying to purge from his system.

"Right, right," he continued. "And what's he doing? Is he looking for her?"

He fell silent again. I strained my ears to see if I could make out what Jake was saying on the other end of the line, but I came up with a blunt-ass nothing. I sighed. This was irritating. Really irritating. I wished that I could just have reached into his head and found out what was going on in there, but I knew that I had to just sit here and piece together what I could from one end of the conversation.

"He's not even started?" Tommy exclaimed. He began to pace again – I could hear the sound of his footsteps below, marking out the same agitated pattern as they had done back in my room, and much to my relief, he switched the call to speaker.

"—and he's pretending when he's with the father, but he doesn't seem bothered most of the rest of the time," Jake explained. "Why? You think we should be putting more eyes on him?"

"I think we should try to push him for money," Tommy growled. "Get closer to him. I want to find out what he's hiding."

"No point," Jake replied. "If he wanted to, then he would have gotten involved a long time ago. He doesn't care that she's missing. He's spent most of the time she's been gone with other women, anyway."

"Shit, really?" Tommy replied. He sounded shocked. I knew that I should have been too, but honestly, it didn't surprise me to think of him using my absence to bring women back to the house. At least he wouldn't have to go to the trouble of hiring a hotel room for a night so that I wouldn't find out. Even the thought of him with other women in his bed didn't bother me. Maybe it would have if I had cared about him even one little bit, but I didn't. I never had. I didn't give a single damn what he did or didn't do.

"Yeah, and it looks like he's been enjoying having her out of the picture for just that reason," Jake continued. "I'm going to keep putting pressure on the father; hopefully that'll be enough to get something moving. Why are you so interested in her fiancé, anyway?"

"No reason," he replied. "I've got to go. I'll speak to you later, okay?"

And with that, he hung up the phone, and I figured that it was safe for me to emerge from where I had been listening to him and head downstairs.

He looked up as soon as he heard my footsteps on the stairs; his face dropped when he saw me, and he furrowed his brow.

"How much of that did you hear?" he asked.

I shrugged. "Enough."

He sighed and rubbed a hand over his face.

"Did you know that he'd been cheating on you?"

I nodded.

"Of course I did," I muttered. "It's been going on pretty much the whole time we've been together."

"When was the first time?" he asked, sounding shocked.

"The first time?" I replied, and I cast my mind back to dredge up the memories. In truth, I tried not to think about him at all, and it felt like delving back into some ugly, locked-up part of my brain where I kept all my childhood nightmares.

"The first time was when I couldn't go out because he had left a bruise on my face," I replied. "He wanted someone with him, and so he found a girl to bring."

Tommy's face tightened. I could see the anger in his eyes. But for once, it didn't scare me. Normally, seeing a man pissed like that would have sent a shock of fear down my spine, pushed me to that place where I would do anything I could to placate him, but I knew I didn't have to worry about that with him. He was kinder than that, kinder than anyone I had ever met before. A man who could look at everything that I had been through and see that it hadn't been my fault.

"I'm so sorry you had to go through that," he told me, finally, his voice edged with sadness. He took a step towards me and wrapped his arms around me tight, pulling me in close to him and letting me lean against his shoulder.

And his touch – his touch was everything that I needed. Even though he was angry right now, he was making sure that he didn't take it out on me – he knew that it wasn't my fault, and he was never going to treat me as though it was. I was so grateful that it almost made tears spring to my eyes, but I managed to hold them back. I couldn't remember the last time that I had been with someone who had made me feel this cared-for, this safe.

And he was the man who had kidnapped me. I shouldn't be feeling anything but hatred for him. And yet...

This had all started because I wanted to make a phone call. But I could tell that it had turned into something far deeper than that. I knew that it was real, whatever was here between us. I cared for him, deeply. I felt something between us that burned with an intensity that I had never felt before in my life. Knowing that he wanted to protect me, knowing that he didn't blame me for everything that had happened with Matt – the relief was almost more than I could take, a physical weight off of my shoulders.

"Thank you," he murmured to me, and I pulled back to look at him with surprise.

"Thank you?" I repeated. He nodded.

"What for?" I wondered aloud.

"Thank you for being honest with me," he told me, and he smoothed my hair back from my face and cupped my chin in his hand.

"I know that it can't have been easy for you. Thank you for telling me the truth."

I nodded. I didn't know what else to say to him. Honestly, the emotion was catching in my throat just hearing him say that, and I didn't really think I could talk anyway.

I was glad that I had finally found someone I could be honest with, someone who wouldn't judge me for everything that I had been through. Even if I would be torn from him eventually, even if my real life was going to catch up with me soon, I wanted to enjoy the freedom of knowing that I didn't have to keep anything from him.

For now.

Chapter Twenty

Tommy

I WAS GOING TO KILL him.

It was the only thing that I had been able to think since she had told me everything that he had put her through. I couldn't let a man like that be in the world for a moment longer, knowing the harm he could inflict on innocent people – knowing the harm that he had inflicted on her.

Because the thought of him laying so much as a hand on her was enough to make my stomach twist with a burning rage that I had never felt before in my life. I wanted to find him and kick the shit out of him. I wanted to grab him by the collar and demand to know why he had promised to marry her when he clearly didn't care about her at all.

I knew the answer to that question, though. He knew that marrying her would solidify his position with her father, that they would never turn against him as long as he could call her his wife. It was sick, twisted, the way that he had played that game, but that didn't mean that it wouldn't work. I couldn't count how many women I had seen over the years, trapped in these marriages with men who clearly saw them as nothing more than pieces on a chessboard that they could move around at will. I didn't want that for her. I didn't want that for anyone. But I knew that I couldn't let Charlotte go back to that life.

I had been in the study all afternoon, trying to order my thoughts. I knew that I would have to start somewhere with all of this, have to find an approach that worked for me. I needed to take him out, that was for sure, but I also needed to get her away from the situation that she had been stuck in that had led her to be engaged to such a vile man. How could nobody around her have suspected anything? Did they really just cover their eyes and pretend that they didn't see the bruises, the fear, the way she flinched when someone raised their voice around her?

The only question was whether she wanted to go. That was what I needed to work out. Maybe there were parts of the life that she wanted to stick with, even if I couldn't for the life of me work out what they were. Just because she had been through this shit with that awful man didn't mean that she hated everything about that world. I needed to remember that. If I was going to get her out, it was going to be because she wanted out, not because some other man had just come into her life and told her what she was going to do with it...

There was a knock at the door, and it opened to reveal Charlotte standing on the other side, carrying a couple of plates.

"You've been in here a while," she explained as she handed me one of them. It was a little charcuterie board, with some meats, cheese, bread, and fruit. "I thought you could use something to eat." She planted herself down in the seat opposite me and eyed me nervously. I knew that she must have had a million questions as to what I had been doing, but honestly, I wasn't sure if she wanted to hear the answer.

"Is everything okay?" she asked. I nodded.

"Everything's fine."

"You've just been acting...different, ever since I told you about everything that's going on with my...with Matt," she explained. Every time she said his name, it was as though she was exorcising a demon from her system. I hated it. I hated the way it sounded on her lips. She shouldn't have had to go through this, not again – and I wasn't going to ask her to. I was going to lift the weight of this from her shoulders.

"I've been thinking," I began, and she cocked an eyebrow at me. The curiosity shimmered in her eyes, and I couldn't help but smile at the sight of it. Fuck, she was gorgeous, so beautiful that it made my chest ache. I needed to get her out of this mess that she had been trapped in. I needed to, one way or the other, no matter how hard it was.

"What do you think of your life with your father?" I began. She furrowed her brow at me.

"How do you mean?"

"Do you like it?" I asked. "All of it, I mean. Even before Matt came along. What's it like?"

She sighed, reached for a piece of bread, and began shredding it absently onto the plate as she considered what I had just said to her.

"Honestly, no," she confessed. "It's not – I know a lot of people would kill to have had all the opportunities that I've had, to live in the kind of luxury I've been in for my entire life, but honestly...I just never wanted any of it. Not really. It was never really my thing, and I don't want to – I mean, it's so much pressure..."

She trailed off for a moment, almost seeming surprised by what had come out of her mouth. I nodded at her, telling her to keep going. This was good. This was what I needed to hear from her. That she was struggling, that she wanted out, for more reasons than just her waste-of-space fiancé.

"It's all about keeping up appearances," she explained. "It's all about making sure that I don't do or say the wrong thing and hurt someone or let someone think that my family doesn't like them, or – or worse, they might think that my father is out to get them if I'm anything other than totally sweet to them. That's what I can't stand. This feeling like everything I do has this huge significance, even when I'm just trying to live my life."

"Would you want to get out?" I asked her. "If you could?"

"I would love to," she replied, snorting with amusement at the thought of it. "But—"

"I want to get you out."

She fell silent. Dead silent. Her eyes were wide as she pinned them on me.

"What the hell did you just say?" Her voice was edged with shock, but there was something else there, too – something like hope, something that made my whole body light up. She wanted this. She might not have been able to put it into words quite yet, but she wanted it just the same way that I did.

"I want to get you out of there," I told her. "Get you away from Matt. And out of your father's grip, if you want it. I don't want to have to send you back to live that life, it's not – it's not fair."

She didn't say a word. Her eyes were wide with shock, and I could see a million questions, a million doubts, a million things that she could have used to undercut my idea rushing around her brain right now.

But she didn't come out with any of them. Because she knew. She knew that this was what she wanted, too, as hard as it might have been to come out and say that, even to herself.

"You can't just do that," she replied, shaking her head. "My father, he's looking for me right now. And—"

"And he hasn't found you yet," I pointed out. All of this was starting to come together inside my head, and I could almost taste her freedom on my tongue. I wanted more. I wanted to take it further. I needed to. For her. I would never let her get hurt again...

"You'll get yourself killed," she told me bluntly. "And what about your brother? You have a whole family business of own, you know, you can't just—"

"I don't want anything to do with it anymore," I replied. "I never have, not really. This has always been Jake's thing. If I could get out, know that I would never have to come back, then I would do it in an instant."

"Then why haven't you done it before?" she asked me, eyeing me.

"Because I've never had a reason to before now," I replied, and I reached over the table and took her hand. I could see the doubt in her eyes, but she had no reason to doubt me. I could do this. I could get both of us out of here, and that was the only thing in the world that mattered right now. I could see straight through to the other side, to the other side of a life that both of us could live together. We could escape. Start over. Be new people, gone from the messes that our families had tried to make of us...

"You'd spend the rest of your life looking over your shoulder," she pointed out, "wondering when the penny was going to drop. Because you know as well as I do that you don't just get to opt out of this shit when you feel like you've had enough. Otherwise there would be a hell of a lot more people doing just that as soon as they got the chance."

Her reaction wasn't what I had been hoping for. But I knew she was right. She had good reason to be nervous, to think about what the hell was going to happen if I really did go through with this. But didn't she want it? Didn't she want to escape? We had both been stuck in this world for such a long time now, and there was a part of me that needed that freedom that I had never been afforded until the moment that I had laid eyes on her. We could get out. We could escape. We could start over and begin again and forget that we had ever been stuck in this mess.

"Don't you want it?" I asked her. "To get out, start over?"

"I don't know," she confessed. "I – I know that I don't want to go back to my life the way it is now, but that doesn't mean that I want to..."

She trailed off. There was so much doubt in her eyes right now. I knew that she just needed time to work out what she wanted, and she would be with me every step of the way.

I hoped. Because this idea was the only thing in the world that felt solid in my head right now, and I wasn't going to let go of it for anything. I wanted to get out of here, and I wanted to do it with her – I wanted to escape the lives that we had both been trapped in for so long, and I could tell that she wanted it, too. We just needed to take that one step forward, the step that would finally let us tip over the edge and into the freedom we so clearly needed. I squeezed her hand tight in mine, hoping that she would see the truth sooner rather than later. The truth of what we were meant to be. The way we were meant to live.

And the freedom that we were meant to enjoy.

Chapter Twenty-One

Charlotte

I SAT THERE IN THE library, a book open on my lap, hardly able to think about what I was reading.

Because I couldn't stop thinking about Tommy, and what he had said to me when I had come into his study earlier in the day.

Was he serious? He seemed to be. He seemed enthused about the whole idea of getting both of us out of here, and honestly, there was a part of me that wanted nothing more than to let go of some of the control that I had been hanging on to and just give in to the freedom that he was offering. I loved the thought of just getting out, getting loose, the way that I had always dreamed of doing.

But it wasn't just about getting out. That was only the first step, and honestly, it would be the easiest one. There was no way that my father was ever going to stop looking for me, especially if he found out that I had made a break for it with someone that had kidnapped me. After all, how the hell could I spin that to him, or to anyone? That I just so happened to have met a man I really felt a connection with after I had been swiped off the street and sequestered away in this house for a few days?

Nobody would ever buy it. Hell, I wasn't even sure if I did. Surely, this was too good to be true. There was no way that I could just stick around and let this happen. Yes, I liked him, yes, I thought he was cool, but how in the hell was I going to convince anyone that this was real?

People were going to judge me. And when I got pulled back to my old life, they were going to think I was crazy. Not to mention what would happen with Matt when he found out…Oh, shit, even the thought of that was enough to make my entire stomach tense with fear. He would rip the world apart before he would let me be with another man, even though he had probably had ten women rotating through his bed since the moment he'd realized that I wasn't going to be home anytime soon.

He would ruin my life. And the worst part was I didn't think anyone would be there to stop him any longer. After this, if I ran, if I tried to get away, people would think that I was better off locked up and stuck with him than I was out on my own. I would be the story that women like me whispered between themselves, warning each other not to get too free with what they did or what they dreamed of…

Or maybe I could be a different kind of story. A story with a happy ending. A promise that, no matter where you had started in life, there was always hope that you could find freedom…

But that wasn't even considering what Tommy was going to go through with his brother. He was stuck with him, really – from what I could tell, they were each other's only family, and Jake would do whatever he had to be the top dog. I could see Tommy in a million different worlds to this one, enjoying a million different lives, but his brother? His brother would always have come back to this, to this darkness, this cruelty. It was in his blood. I could sense it whenever I was around him, and it always made me feel sick with fear.

I knew he was coming back to the house that day, and I knew that I was going to have to head back to my room and lock myself up in there just to keep out of his way. I didn't want to deal with anything from him, not when my head was already so stuffed-full of everything that I had to do, everything that I had to think about.

When I heard the tires crunching on the gravel outside, I tucked the book under my arm and hurried for the door. I didn't want to get Tommy into trouble.

I felt as though everyone would be able to guess what we had been planning from the first moment that he had spoken it out loud. As though he would accidentally spread it to the universe at large just by saying it. I knew that he was putting himself in danger, and that he had to put a whole hell of a lot of trust in me not to tell his brother or anyone else what he had been planning...

He trusted me. As I closed the bedroom door behind me and leaned back against it, that thought caught me off guard. He really must have trusted me if he had been willing to share that with me. It had been a long time since I felt like I had earned anyone's trust in me, but to know that he had been so willing to gift it to me – that was something that I was never going to forget.

I knew that what he was saying was a fantasy. I knew that the chances of pulling it off were virtually nil, and that we might end up caught or worse in the process. But if something as simple as someone actually trusting me made me feel the way that it did, could I really afford to pass up the chance to get out?

I wanted to get out of there, and I wanted to do it with him. I wanted his freedom as much as I wanted mine – I wanted him to have the chance to escape the world that he had been trapped in, just the same way that I had been. I hadn't expected this when I had first been taken, but maybe there was something to be said for giving in to the sweetness and the promise of everything that he had laid out in front of me. Maybe...

I could hear chaos downstairs, shouting, stomping around, and I knew that Jake was back. I didn't know how Tommy had wound up burdened with such a piece of shit for a brother, but he deserved to get out from under his thumb as much as I did. When he asked me to leave with him, he was asking for my permission as much as he was my agreement. Asking for someone to enjoy this time with him, to stand with him while he made a run for it, once and for all.

And that person was going to be me. It had to be. I couldn't deny it any longer. I had to get out of here and I had to get him out of here, too. We needed to do this. We were going to do this. The flood of excitement hit me so hard that I nearly forgot about the shouting downstairs, and it wasn't until I heard the front door slam loudly that I came back into my body once more.

I hurried over to my bed as I made out footsteps coming up the stairs. If it was Jake coming to check on me, then I needed to make sure that I didn't have the book visible. He would want to know where I had gotten it from, and I didn't want to dump Tommy in the shit for just giving me a little freedom.

But instead, there was a knock at my door, and I got up to answer it. I knew that Jake would never have knocked, so it had to be Tommy. And sure enough, as soon as I opened it, I smiled as I saw him standing on the other side.

"Are you okay?" I asked him as he brushed past me and into the room before someone could see him. He nodded.

"Jake's back," he growled. "Swinging his dick around again."

"Is he close?" I asked, worried that he might have spotted Tommy coming into the room. Tommy shook his head.

"No, he's outside with the guards," he replied. "He's not going to stay there long, though. I just had to see you."

He slipped his hand down my arm and linked his fingers with my own, and I swear, the sweetness of that touch was almost enough to make me swoon on the spot. How was it that he could be this sweet and tender with me, when he was dealing with the stress of everything that his brother was throwing at him?

He leaned over to plant a kiss on my lips, and I kissed him back, knowing that these stolen moments were all that we were going to get until we got out of here. As he pulled back and looked into my eyes, I knew that I had to tell him.

"I want to leave with you," I blurted out finally, and he stared at me for a moment, taking in what I had just said.

"You want to...?"

"I want to leave with you," I explained. "It's been – I know that it's going to be hard, but we can't stay here. Neither of us can. We need to get out, I can see that now. We have to escape."

The shock in his eyes soon mellowed into something else entirely, a surprised joy that spread all the way to the huge smile that appeared on his face.

"You really mean it?" he asked, and I nodded. I meant it. I wasn't sure how much else I could say, how much more time we had left before his brother was going to come busting the door down and tell him to get away from me, but I knew that I had to do this. It was what we needed, what we both deserved, and I wasn't going to let anything get in the way of it.

"I mean it," I replied, and he kissed me again. I knew it was risky, but I wished that I could steal just a few more moments with him.

"Thank you," he murmured, and he lifted my hands to his lips and kissed them softly. "I have to go. But I – we'll talk about all of this soon, okay? Just as soon as I've gotten my brother out of the way."

"I know," I replied, nearly giddy with the thrill of what I had just agreed do. And with one last smile, he slipped out of the door and down the hallway. I knew that the conversation we'd just exchanged was going to change everything. And I couldn't wait to find out how my life was about to shift now that I had agreed to get out with him.

I sank down on to the edge of the bed and stared at the small window that led back to the outside world. Soon, I promised myself – soon, I would be out, and I would have the freedom I'd always dreamed of.

Chapter Twenty-Two

Jake

I LOOKED DOWN THE LIST that I had made, everything that I had managed to pull together about the men who worked here, and I knew that I was going to have to do better if I was going to get us out of here in one piece.

The last two days had been entirely built around putting in motion the plan that I had formed with Charlotte. We needed to get out, and that meant that I was going to have to find at least a couple of guys who would be willing to cover for us in the first few days of our absence. It wasn't going to be easy, that was for sure, but I knew that I could pull it off.

I had started canvassing the guards at the house, figuring out if I could trust them – figuring out how far they were willing to turn on Jake to help me get what I wanted. I knew that I couldn't be the only one who hated my brother enough to want to fuck him over, but, so far, it seemed like he had scared the majority of them into submission. They weren't talking. And they weren't about to start now.

"What do you think of her?" I had prompted one of them, Andrew, as he stood at watch at the front door. He shrugged.

"Like to get my hands on her," he replied, flashing me a grin. I clenched my fist at my side. I knew that they must have noticed her beauty, too, but I was surprised that they would be so willing to say it to me. After all, I was as much a part of this as Jake was, but they clearly didn't see me in the same way that they saw him. Which could help in some ways, but I hated how confident they were in telling me shit like that.

I hadn't been able to find anyone who seemed willing to really go against Jake – not that I had asked them outright, too worried that it might give away what I was planning. All it had confirmed was that I seriously didn't want to leave Charlotte alone with these creeps if I could avoid it. I wondered if I had been the only thing between her and one of them doing something awful this entire time...

But before I could get too caught up in that, Jake strode out of the kitchen and right up to me. I could tell from the way he was walking, before I so much as lifted my gaze to look at him, that he was in a good mood.

"Ransom negotiations," Jake told me. "Tonight. In the city. You're coming with me."

My eyes widened.

"What?"

"You heard me," he replied. "We have to get moving on this. Her father and her man are meeting with us later tonight. We need to be there."

"And you don't think they're trying to set us up?" I asked. I needed to find a way out of this. I didn't want to leave her alone in this place, not if I could help it, and honestly, the thought of being so far from her was enough to make my stomach churn.

"I think they'll do anything they can to get her back," he replied, grinning at me, as though he was delivering the best news in the world. "We can leave her here for a night. The guards can cope."

"You trust them?" I asked, narrowing my eyes at him.

"I trust them because they know that if they lay a finger on her, they're dead," he replied. Loudly enough that I was sure anyone around us could hear it. As though he might just have had reason to doubt them, too.

"Fine," I muttered. At least I could stall the meeting a little, keep track of how things were going to go. Even if the thought of seeing that monster Matt in person made me want to punch a wall.

I agreed to go with Jake and took off to see Charlotte as soon as I got the chance. She sounded terrified when I told her what I was planning to do.

"You can't go," she pleaded with me. "You have to stay here, please. You don't know what they'll do—"

"I need to," I told her gently. "And I'll be back soon, I promise. Lock your doors tonight, okay? Don't let anyone in unless it's me."

"What – am I in danger?" she asked me. I shook my head, even though it was a lie. I didn't know what those guards might do with the freedom of having Jake out of the house.

"Just a precaution," I assured her. "Stay safe, okay? Don't worry. I'll be back as soon as I can..."

She kissed me before I left, and I wished that I could tell Jake right then and there that I was getting out and that there was nothing he could do to get me to stay. But I didn't have that choice, not now, not yet. Too dangerous to make a run for it...

Jake insisted on driving us to the city, and I watched as the road passed us by, every moment in this car taking me farther and farther away from her.

By the time we got to the meet-up point, I could see that Jake was practically vibrating with excitement. This was the shit that he liked best, when he could pretend that he was just as much a gangster as our father had been. I hated it, personally, because I never knew when things could take a turn for the worst – but I supposed that's what Jake hoped for. He wanted that shift to come, that change to hit, the guns to be pulled out. No doubt right now he was imagining some showdown where he got to take out the most powerful crime boss in the city, no matter how far removed from reality that was.

Jake strode in without spending a second readying me for what was to come, and I hustled my ass to keep up. Inside the small safehouse – supposedly neutral ground – Charlotte's father and her fiancé were waiting for us behind a desk. Her father was sitting down, Matt standing there. As I locked eyes with Matt for the first time, I had to clench my fists at my sides to keep from taking a swing at him. Did her father have any clue of the hurt that he had caused his daughter?

"So you made it," her father greeted Jake with an icy tone to his voice. Jake crossed his arms over his chest and eyed him in a way that he likely thought made him look like a badass. In truth, he was more a petulant teenager, but I wasn't going to be the one to break it to him.

"Where is she?" he demanded. Jake snorted with laughter as he took a seat at the desk; I stayed standing, just like Matt was, the two of us mirror images of each other. I glared at him, wishing that I could spit at his feet, show him how much I fucking hated him, but I knew I had to play it cool for now. This was just talk. Hopefully, no agreements would be made, and I could keep Charlotte back at that house without anything to worry about for a little while longer.

"She's in our safehouse," Jake replied.

"I wanted to see her," he snapped back. "I need to know that she's unharmed—"

"She's fine," Jake replied, shaking his head. "Trust me, your daughter's a lot more *resilient* than you might think she is. Doesn't have any trouble keeping a bed warm on a cold night, right?"

Matt bristled. Not that he had any fucking right to. I knew that he had been bringing girls through his house like he wasn't engaged to one of the most beautiful women in the state.

"But she's unharmed?" Lou pressed. Jake nodded again.

"We've made sure of that," he replied. At least I knew that he was telling the truth with that part of it. I wasn't going to let anything happen to her. Never. Even if it meant keeping her from her father.

"Good," he sighed, rubbing a hand over his face. It was almost surreal, being in a room with a man who had all the power that he did, but I didn't let it get to me. I had to remember that he was happy to sell his daughter off to the man beside him. He wasn't a father to her. He was just another man who had used her for what she could give to him.

"So let's talk about money," Jake began, leaning forward. It was clear that he had been planning this in his head since the moment that he'd found out that he was actually going to see Saint-Claire in person. He was speaking fast, making sure that nobody had a chance to keep up with him, probably sensing that, if they did, they would see through his game.

He ran through what they had already talked about, like he was selling some new product on a reality TV channel and knew that he didn't have long to keep his attention. But then, he shifted, forcing the conversation in a new direction that took even me by surprise.

"I need to know that you're serious about getting her back," Jake remarked, narrowing his eyes at Saint-Claire on the other side of the table. "You have to understand, there are plenty of people who would pay for her. If you want to convince us that you're the ones we should go with..."

"I'm her father," Lou growled, clearly furious. "I'm the only one she belongs to. And I'm going to do anything I can to get her back."

"We've had some offers," Jake went on, trying to keep his voice calm. I could sense the nerves right now – he knew that we hadn't had any other offers, and that I wouldn't have let him even entertain them if we had. She wasn't some product to be bounced around between whoever could afford her. She was a person. A human being. Who needed protection from this sick world.

"And we need you to match them, or better them," he continued.

"How much?" he barked back. Jake hit him with a number that made even me raise my eyebrows.

The amount he was asking for would put a major dent in Saint-Claire's fortune. And in his influence, too. More to the point, though, it would consolidate Jake's power. And that was what scared me the most. I knew that he couldn't be given anything more than what he already had, or else he was going to shoot into some stratosphere of arrogance and influence that would lead him to some dark places.

But instead of arguing, Saint-Claire just nodded.

"If that's what it takes to get her back," he replied, and his voice cracked. For an instant, I almost believed that he really cared about his daughter, but then my eyes slid to Matt beside him, and I knew that he couldn't. If he did, he would never have allowed someone like that anywhere close to her. Not in a million years.

"Glad to hear it," Jake replied, a smile spreading out over his face. And just like that, our meeting was over.

Jake insisted on looping around the city a few times to throw off anyone who might have been following us before we headed back to the house, but I couldn't focus on his paranoia right now. No, the only thing that I could think of was that number – the amount that he had asked for, how much it was going to change things. Jake would be able to do anything he wanted. And that was bad news.

By the time that we got back to the house, my head was spinning with the implications of everything that had happened. This was going to be a mess. I was going to have to fight to keep Jake's head on straight if he really did get that money – but more than anything, it was going to make it even harder to handle everything that Charlotte was going through. Jake didn't want to keep her around any longer than he had to, and if that meant handing her off as soon as he got the money, he would do it.

Time was running out. And I knew I had to act fast if I was going to save her from the mess of what her life had been before.

As soon as I stepped out of the car, I heard a commotion inside the house. Fear pulsing through me, I took the steps two at a time to get to her. Shoving the door open with a bang, I looked up the stairs to see that very same guard that I had spoken to, Andrew, staggering back from her room in shock.

"Fucking bitch!" he yelled at her, and I sprinted toward him, grabbing him by the collar and pulling him to his feet.

"What the fuck did you do?" I snarled at him. His eyes seemed to tense with terror for a moment, as though he knew what was going to happen next.

"Nothing," he blurted out, and I dropped him to his knees again and hurried toward her room.

She was sitting in the doorway, slumped down against it, staring off into space. I leaned down to her, putting my arms around her without even pausing to think about how this might look to anyone who saw us.

"What happened?" I asked her, though I was sure I already knew. She looked up at me, eyes distant, as though she was on another planet.

"He tried to get in," she replied, vaguely waving her hand in the direction of that man.

"Are you okay?" I demanded, and she nodded.

"Yeah, I'm fine," she replied. She didn't even seem that shaken. And it hurt to know that it was likely because she had dealt with far worse at the hands of the man she was going to marry.

I guided her to her feet again, put my arm around her, and led her to her bed to rest. I could already hear Jake berating Andrew, and I knew it wouldn't be long till he took care of him for good. But all I cared about now was making sure that she stayed safe – making sure that she had nothing to fear. As long as I was here, she was going to be okay. And I needed her to know I would never renege on that.

Chapter Twenty-Three

Charlotte

I STARED AT THE BLANK wall opposite me, trying to ground myself again. I'd heard the gunshot the night before, I knew that the man who had tried to break in here was gone, and I knew that Tommy wouldn't let anything happen to me.

But that didn't mean that I wasn't scared.

I hadn't slept a wink the night before, too consumed with the dark thoughts of what he would have done to me if I hadn't kicked him between the legs playing on my mind. I knew the darkness that men were capable of, I knew the cruelty that they could inflict, especially when they had you captive.

Tommy had been with me for a while, but it hadn't taken long for Jake to notice that his brother was paying a little too much attention to me, and he had to leave. He had promised that he would be back the first chance he got, but I still hadn't been able to sleep for fear of something else happening...

I listened to the car tires crunching on the gravel and prayed that it was Jake leaving again. I knew that he likely had to deal with my father, and I wanted him gone so that I could be with Tommy, the only man who really made me feel safe.

I heard the door creak and lifted my head to see him coming towards me. Relief hit me hard, and I sat up and reached out for him. He wound his arms around me, sinking down on to the edge of the bed and planting a kiss on my cheek as he did so.

"Fuck, I'm so glad to see you," he murmured against my neck.

"Me too," I breathed. "I thought – I wasn't sure if my father would even let you come back in one piece."

"He did," he replied. "And he's made a deal with Jake. Better than I thought it would go, actually. But I'm not happy about it."

"Why, what happened?" I asked, nervous. I had to control myself. I didn't want to say or do something that would let him see my nerves.

"He's accepted the offer that Jake gave to him," Tommy explained. "And it looks like he wants you back sooner rather than later. It's...a lot of money he's paying for you. He really seems to want you safe."

I sank my head down on to his shoulder. I felt awful for doing this to my father, but I didn't know how else I could put it right. I wanted to be there for my father, I did, I didn't want to have to ignore him like this. But if I even gave him a hint that I was going to come back, then he would lock me away in the life that he had wanted for me since I was a little girl.

The life that would stick me with Matt.

"I don't want to leave him like that," I muttered. The guilt stirring in me hurt. I knew that my father only wanted the best for me, but still...

"You can't let that get in the way," he told me, cupping my face in his hand and looking me in the eyes. "We have to get out. You know that, right?"

"I know," I agreed. And I meant it. I hadn't agreed to come with him for no reason. He smoothed my hair back from my face.

"What happened last night?" he murmured. I had been trying my hardest not to think about it, but I was scared to say it out loud. I shook my head.

"It doesn't matter—"

"It does," he replied softly. "I know it's hard for you to think about it, but was anyone else involved?"

"No, I think it was just him," I admitted. "I – I didn't really have a chance to think about it. He kicked the door open, and he told me that he – he told me that while you were out, he was going to…"

I tried to push it to the back of my mind. I didn't want to deal with this. I had seen the look in his eyes, and I had known at once what he was getting at.

And it scared me fucking shitless.

"You're safe, you're safe," he murmured, rubbing the small of my back gently. "You have nothing to worry about with me, okay?"

"I know," I breathed, closing my eyes and trying to gather myself. "But it was just him, that's what I remember," I assured him once I had managed to ground myself once more. "I don't think any of the other guards had anything to do with it."

"Good, good," he muttered. "I'm trying to work out which ones we can actually trust at the moment. I know that we're going to need some on our side if we're going to get out of here in one piece. We just need to make sure that we don't tap any of the ones who would have gone along with what had happened to you."

"Hell, no," I replied, shivering at the thought. The mere notion of what he might have done to me if I hadn't kneed him in the nuts and made it out of the room made my head spin.

But it hadn't happened like that, that's what I needed to keep reminding myself. I was still the one in control here; I was still the one who had fought him off. I might not even have bothered if it hadn't been for Tommy, but knowing that he was keeping me around, knowing that he was here for me – that was all that I needed to stand up for myself. All that I needed to convince myself that I was worth protecting.

"What are we going to do?" I asked. "How long before we make a run for it?"

"I need to get the guards in place before we do anything like that," he warned me. "But I know we have to move fast. Your father can move a lot of money around pretty fast, and I don't want to give him the chance to get where he needs to be – Jake's going to want you out of our hands as soon as he possibly can. He's going to get you out of here whenever that money lands in his account. And then he'll take you back..."

He trailed off, as though the mere thought of it was more than he could possibly deal with. I knew that it was for me. The thought of everything that was waiting for me back there, everything that was happening, was enough to make the hairs on the back of my neck stand up.

"I've spoken to some of the guards this morning, told them what happened to you last night, and I think I might have something to work with," he went on. "They were pissed when I told them what happened, and I could tell that they wanted you to be safe. That might be enough for us to base something on."

"But are they really going to go against Jake?" I wondered aloud. "After everything that's happened?"

"I don't know," he sighed. "We're not going to know until we bite the bullet and actually do this or don't."

"I know," I agreed. And I knew, too, that I was taking such a huge risk even thinking about making a run for it with this man, but I also knew, clear as day, that there was no way in hell that I was going to back off now. I had come so far. I had met someone who made me feel alive in a way that I never had before – someone so far outside of the realm of anything I'd known before that it felt like a whole new world.

I had to chase this through. I had to get out of here and it had to be with him – it had to be with someone else who was going to understand what I was running from, and why I was running from it. We had come into each other's lives for a reason, and I would be damned if I let that go.

Chapter Twenty-Four

Tommy

"HAVE YOU GOT EVERYTHING?" I asked Charlotte.

"I have nothing to take with me," she pointed out, offering me a slightly nervous smile. I could tell that she was struggling with the thought of making a run for it, but she knew it's what we had to do. We had to get out of there. And we couldn't turn back once we had officially made a run for it.

Anyway. I knew that we had a couple of days till Jake got back from the city – he was putting together the final pieces of the puzzle of the deal he had made with Charlotte's father, and then he would be back to pick her up and bring her home.

Not home. Wherever we were going, that was going to be home. I had to keep reminding myself of that.

"How long do you think we have before he gets back?" she asked, and I shook my head.

"A couple of days yet," I assured her. "We'll be far away by the time he gets here, I promise."

"And what about the guards?"

"I have one who's willing to turn a blind eye to us getting out," I explained. "He's got a daughter about your age – I think he just wants to see you out of all this as much as I do."

"Good," she breathed. I knew that she was scared shitless right now – this was the closest she had ever come to getting away from everything that she had been trapped in till this point, and I knew that it must have been a headfuck to think about everything that she was doing. She'd been locked in her gilded cage for so many years, the thought of escaping must have seemed impossible. But here we were. About to go.

Tonight.

"I just need to pack the car with some stuff and we can get out of here," I promised her, and I leaned over her bed to give her a kiss on the lips. She grasped my face for a moment, looking me deep in the eye.

"You're not going to leave me, are you?" she asked fearfully. I shook my head at once.

"I'm not going to leave you here," I promised her. "I want out of this as much as you do, okay? That's just the way it is. I won't leave you here. We're in this together."

"Thank you," she sighed, and she pulled back from me. "Okay, go, go. We have to hurry..."

And then, I saw the look on her face as she clocked the noise that was coming from outside. A car. A vehicle. Shit – and it sounded like Jake's.

"Is that...?" she murmured.

"Stay here," I told her, and I dived for the door so that I could intercept Jake before he got upstairs. I needed him to stay away from her. I thought we'd have more time before he got back – thought at least we could get a good hundred miles away before he rolled up again, but clearly, we were going to have no such luck. I sprinted downstairs and managed to catch him before he came in.

"Well, good morning!" he slurred, lifting up a half-empty bottle of vodka. I grimaced. I hated him when he had been drinking. More than I usually hated him, at least.

"Thought we could do some celebrating," he announced as he grabbed me and tossed his arm around my shoulders. "Get that little girlfriend of yours down from her room, might as well enjoy her while she's still here, right?"

"What are you talking about?"

"The deal's all but done," he explained as he staggered towards the kitchen to get a glass. "She's going to be their problem soon. Might as well make the most of her..."

The way he was talking about her made me sick. Even sicker, though, was how close I had been to making it out of here before my fucking brother turned up out of the blue to throw a wrench into the works. Of course he had fucked it up for me – when hadn't he?

Still. At least I could keep Charlotte around right now – he was drunk enough that he wouldn't have noticed if she had been sitting on my lap the entire time. I headed upstairs to grab her, my mind racing as I tried to work out what to do next...

As I knocked on her door again, it hit me. Drink him under the table. Take a couple of shots, let him think that I was down to celebrate like he was, and get him blackout drunk. When she opened the door, I took her hand and squeezed it tight.

"Change of plans," I told her swiftly. "He's here. But he's drunk as hell. He wants us to drink with him, keep him company – if we do that, we can get him to black out and then make a run for it. Okay?"

"Okay," she replied, but she looked spooked. Any slight shift in the plan must have been enough to convince her that I was having second thoughts. I grabbed her by the waist, pulled her close to me, and kissed her hard. When I pulled back, her eyes stayed shut for a split second, as though she was still lingering in that moment. And then she smiled at me.

"Okay," she repeated, but this time with a huskier edge to her voice that told me she was ready to do whatever it took to see this thing through.

I guided her downstairs, where Jake was pouring drinks for all of us – he must have just avoided the cops driving home, given how drunk he was right now. I hated the thought of him hurting someone else because of his reckless bullshit, but I knew that the time had long-passed to try and hold him to account for all the irresponsible shit that he got up to.

"There she is, woman of the hour," Jake announced, lifting his glass to Charlotte and then shoving one in her direction. She looked at me, and I nodded slightly, giving her permission to drink. We had to make sure that he thought we were right there along with him, or he would start to suspect something, and that was the last thing we needed.

"You have no idea how much money you're going to make us, Charlotte, baby," Jake crooned to her as he handed me a glass. I stiffened. The way he was talking to her, something had changed. Maybe it was just because he thought he could do whatever he wanted to her with no repercussions, but I wasn't going to let that happen. I moved back by her side, and she shriveled against me, clearly as bothered by his strange come-ons as I was.

I didn't want him even fucking looking at her. She had been through enough at his hands already. And no matter what happened, he was still my brother. If he did something to her that I couldn't stop, then she would always look at me as the one who hadn't been able to control him. I wasn't going to let that happen. Not a chance in hell. Not when I had come so far – not when I was so close to getting to where we needed to be.

He rambled on about how much we were going to make, and Charlotte and I pretended to sip on our drinks as we watched him get drunker and drunker. His sheer arrogance took even me by surprise – I hadn't expected him to come out swinging as such an idiot in all of this, so sure that he could just get hammered and still pull this off. He might be almost done, but he should have known from years of watching our father work that it was these last few steps were everything could go terribly, horribly wrong. If he wasn't careful, he was going to lose what he so clearly thought he already had.

And I was going to be the one to take it from him.

As he got drunker and drunker, he became more and more lecherous to the woman standing beside me. Up until now, it was as though he couldn't even see her, but all of a sudden, he was acting like he had been into her all this time. The two of us had always had a similar taste in women, so this hardly came as a surprise to me, but I thought he had nothing but contempt for her. Nothing but jealousy that she had been born into a crime family that he would never be able to get close to. Clearly, I had been wrong.

"You're a beautiful woman, Charlotte," he slurred as he shifted a little closer to her. I tensed, hoping that he could sense it and would back off, but he was getting too drunk for that now. Which was a good sign for our plan in the long-term, but a bad one in the immediate. She pulled back from him again.

"If you didn't have a fiancé, I'd be trying to marry you myself," he went on. "Think about how good-looking our kids would be..."

"I'd rather not," she shot back, clearly too tired of putting up with his shit to even entertain it anymore. He busted out laughing, as though the whole thing was wildly amusing to him.

"Good one," he chuckled, and he went to get another drink. As soon as his back was turned, she pulled a face at me. I mouthed *I'm sorry* at her and hoped that he would lay off soon. I didn't want to have to keep making excuses for this fucker. Though I had to keep reminding myself that it wouldn't be long until I was done with him for good, and I would never have to put up with his disgusting attempts to hit on the woman I cared for so deeply ever again.

He was stumbling-drunk now, enough that I was surprised he could even stand upright. I had been tossing my drink down the sink every chance that I got, and I was sure that we wouldn't have to wait much longer till he was down for the count.

"I'm hungry," he muttered. "I need something to eat..."

"You need to go to bed," I replied, trying to keep my voice jovial and hoping that he wouldn't read anything into it.

"I need food," he snapped back, and he started rooting through the cupboards. Shit. I needed him to calm the fuck down and get off to bed soon. I couldn't put up with this much longer.

"I'll go get a takeout menu," I replied tersely. Making sure that Charlotte was all right with a quick nod, I hustled my ass out of the room and down towards the office, hoping against hope that all of this would be over quickly. The last thing I needed right now was to have to put up with any more of his drunken shenanigans.

I headed to the office to find what I was looking for, but before I could get there, I was intercepted by someone. One of the guards, Nate, stepped out in front of me, locked eyes with me.

"I hear that the deal's nearly done," he replied. I stared at him for a moment.

"Yes, so?"

"So we'll be expecting our cut soon."

I snorted with laughter.

"Talk to Jake about that," I told him flippantly. "See how far you get trying to convince him to part with any of that cash."

"That's why we've come to you," he went on, slowly, carefully.

"Who's we?"

"The guards who've been doing your dirty work," he replied. "And we deserve some of the cut."

"Jake'll pay you for your time," I shot back. "You have nothing to worry about—"

"We don't want time," he replied, and he took a step towards me, closing the distance between us. I met his gaze steadily, not letting him spook me.

"We want a cut," he continued. "A cut of the money, or a cut of the girl. Your choice."

"What the fuck are you talking about—"

But before I could take him to task for what he had just said, he grabbed my collar and thrust me back against the wall. I struggled to push him off, but he was stronger than me.

"We saw what happened to Andrew, but we figured you couldn't do the same with all of us," he growled. Suddenly, I noticed another pair of men behind him – two more guards, neither of them the one who had agreed to help me. Dread pulsed up my spine. I couldn't handle this. I thought that I only had to deal with Jake tonight, not these fuckers, too.

"So what's it going to be?" he asked, dropping me back to my feet once more. "The money or the girl?"

"Fuck you," I spat at him. And, before I could say another word, he swung his fist at me, caught me in the jaw, and sent me spiraling to the ground below.

"Motherfucker," he hissed, and I felt them crowding around me. I knew that they couldn't take me out right here and now. They probably thought they could use me as a bargaining chip against Jake, and they didn't want to lose out on that so soon. But I wasn't going to stand by and let them take her. They could fuck Jake over for all I cared, take his money from him, but they were never going to get anywhere near Charlotte.

"What the fuck is happening?"

Another voice cut through the ringing in my ears – Art, the guard on my side, had emerged into the hallway.

"We told you, we're taking our share," one of them shot back to him. "You had the chance to get in on it. Now, turn around and walk out, old man—"

I heard the cock of a gun. Then dead silence. Something tensed in me, and I managed to pull myself back to my feet once more.

"Get away from him," Art told them, his voice low and full of fury. The gun in his hand was levelled at the ringleader, and I knew that this was the best chance I had to get out of here.

"Tommy, Jake was taking her upstairs the last time I saw them," he barked to me. "You need to get her out of there. Fast."

I headed for the stairs at high speed, trying to ignore the wet trickle of blood down the back of my neck where my head had struck the wall. None of that mattered now – all that mattered was getting her away from my brother before he did something that he wouldn't be able to take back.

Could he have really meant it when he had been making all of those perverted comments about her before? Maybe. Maybe he was drunk enough to think that he could get away with it, sure enough after all the time he had spent building this plan and executing it that he could allow himself this one slip in his vision. Not only would her family kill him for it – but I would, too.

I could hear footsteps upstairs, and I knew that Jake had already taken her to his room – I dived for the door and kicked it open without a moment's pause, and freezing when I saw what was waiting for me on the other side.

Jake, his belt half-unbuckled, was standing over the bed. And Charlotte was before him, stiff with terror, her eyes wide and her face sapped of all color. I wanted to push him out of the way, to pull her into my arms and tell her that everything was going to be okay and that we were going to get out of there, but I knew she wouldn't have believed me. And that it would have given away my plan to Jake before I had time to see it through.

"Get away from her," I warned him, and he grinned, shaking his head at me.

"Hey, there's plenty of her to go around," he replied, leering down at her once more. I couldn't stand the way he was looking at her. How could he talk about her like that? I had known that my brother was an asshole for a long time, but this – this was something else entirely. This was a new layer of darkness, something exposed in him that I had prayed I would never have to see in someone who shared blood with me.

"Don't do this, Jake," I told him, and I took a step toward him. He tensed.

"Stay there," he ordered me. But I wasn't one of his minions. He couldn't just tell me what to do. He might have liked to think he was in control, but he had no idea.

"You're so close to getting it over with," I replied, trying to shift tack and let him think I was on his side. "Why would you blow it now...?"

"Because she's only good if I'm getting a use out of her," he replied, shooting a look down at her, that grin spreading over his face again.

"You'll get the money, and then this'll be over with," I replied. "You don't have to do this—"

"What's your fucking problem?" Jake exploded at me finally. "Why are you so obsessed with her? Jake, she's just some bitch—"

"Don't talk about her like that," I growled, and, finally, I couldn't hold it in any longer. I dived toward him, intent on getting him out of this room and away from her – but before I could, he reached for a gun that he had left on the dresser, and cocked it in his hand.

"I'd be more careful with me, if you know what's good for you," he told me menacingly. The drunkenness seemed to have been replaced by a clarity that scared me. I knew what he was capable of. I knew what he would do if he felt like he had a right to, and I didn't want her to have to deal with it.

The acrid smell of smoke caught my attention – was something happening downstairs? He had been whining about his hunger before. Maybe he had tried to cook something and had forgotten about it...

Too much was happening right now. And all I knew was that I needed to get her out of here before something set this tinderbox to explode.

"What's your problem, Tommy?" He snarled at me. "Don't tell me that you've got feelings for the bitch. She's a ransom, remember? She's just a means to an end..."

"Then don't fuck that up by hurting her," I argued with him. "Her father will kill you, and you won't see a cent of that cash..."

"Oh, and you'd get to live happily ever after with her, would you?" he shot back. I hadn't realized how much he had noticed of the time that I had spent with her – maybe the guards in this house talked more than I thought they did.

"Give me the gun," I ordered him, holding out my hands. "Come on, you're drunk. Just give me the gun and we can wait for the deal to be done with—"

"Why did you try to hit me?" he demanded. "Because you care about her, don't you? She's got you wrapped around her little finger...."

Suddenly, he swung the gun around on her. Charlotte scrambled back on the bed against the headboard, her eyes wide with terror. Panic lanced through me. I had to play this cool, or I was going to get her killed.

I took a step forward, moving between the gun and the woman I loved. I wasn't going to let him hurt her. Not when I had come so far, not when I had gotten so close to getting her out of this.

"Dude, dude," I implored him. "Calm down. You know that we need her in one piece, right? You're not going to fuck this all up just for some bullshit grudge..."

"You don't get to make the rules here," he snapped back. "I do. This was my idea, remember? And if I want to take this little bitch out, then I'm going to do it..."

He narrowed his eyes, waiting for me to move out of the way. I didn't shift a single step. Not a chance in hell I was going to let him do that to her.

"We're so close," I reminded him. "So close. Think about what we can do if we get that money. And that power. What we can do together…"

His eyes started to glaze a little, and the gun drooped an inch or two. I knew that I was getting through to him. At the end of the day, he knew that our father would have wanted us to work together, and that was what I was appealing to right now – this sense that we were better off with each other. That letting someone come between us would be dangerous.

"You're right," he muttered, and he let the gun slump to his side. "We don't let a bitch like that come between us…"

"Do you smell smoke?" Charlotte squeaked. I glanced around at her, trying to tell her with a single look that I was going to deal with that as soon as I got the chance. But right now, I needed to stay in control. I needed to let Jake think that I was on his side.

He wasn't going to let me leave with her, that much I was sure of. Which meant that I was going to have to go to extraordinary lengths to make sure that I could get her out of here. I knew I still had to get her past the guards downstairs, but I could handle them. It was my brother who worried me the most. The one that I had the least control over.

I knew what I had to do. And it was with this sense of calm that I felt myself move to actually take care of it.

I reached out and took the gun from him. His fingers were limp around it, he didn't even want to be holding it anymore, much to my relief. Our eyes locked for a moment, and in that instant, I almost felt sorry for him. He had come so close to doing everything that he wanted to do, and I was about to take that from him before he had the chance to see it through.

"It's me and you," I told him. "You get it?"

"I get it," he replied and reached out to put an arm around me.

He pulled me in close to him. And I let him.

For another moment, it was almost as though everything else had ceased to be. But I knew what I had to do. If I was going to get us out of this situation, then I had to do it now. There was no turning back.

The sound of the gunshot rang in my ears, the shock of it filling my senses. His arm tightened on my back, holding me close. I prayed this would be the end of the mess that my brother had dragged me into.

Once and for all.

THE END

A Dark Mafia Romance Series

Book 1 – Taken By The Mob Boss
Book 2 – Truce With The Mob Boss
Book 3 – Taking Over The Mob Boss
Book 4 – Trouble For The Mob Boss
Book 5 – Tailored By The Mob Boss
Book 6 – Tricking By The Mob Boss

Find Lexy Timms:

LEXY TIMMS NEWSLETTER:
http://eepurl.com/9i0vD
Lexy Timms Facebook Page:
https://www.facebook.com/SavingForever
Lexy Timms Website:
http://www.lexytimms.com

Lexy
Timms
Managing
BOSSES
Book 1-3
BOSS
BOSS
BOSS
FREE
for a
Limited
Time

Want

FREE READS?

Sign up for Lexy Timms' newsletter
And she'll send you updates on new releases,
ARC copies of books and a whole lotta fun!

Sign up for news and updates!
http://eepurl.com/9i0vD

More by Lexy Timms:

FROM BEST SELLING AUTHOR, Lexy Timms, comes a billionaire romance that'll make you swoon and fall in love all over again.

Jamie Connors has given up on men. Despite being smart, pretty, and just slightly overweight, she's a magnet for the kind of guys that don't stay around.

Her sister's wedding is at the foreground of the family's attention. Jamie would be fine with it if her sister wasn't pressuring her to lose weight so she'll fit in the maid of honor dress, her mother would get off her case and her ex-boyfriend wasn't about to become her brother-in-law.

Determined to step out on her own, she accepts a PA position from billionaire Alex Reid. The job includes an apartment on his property and gets her out of living in her parent's basement.

Jamie must balance her life and somehow figure out how to manage her billionaire boss, without falling in love with him.

** The Boss is book 1 in the Managing the Bosses series. All your questions won't be answered in the first book. It may end on a cliff hanger.

For mature audiences only. There are adult situations, but this is a love story, NOT erotica.

Book 1 – Payment for Sin
Book 2 – Atonement Within
Book 3 – Declaration of Love

Faking It Description:

HE GROANED. THIS WAS torture. Being trapped in a room with a beautiful woman was just about every man's fantasy, but he had to remember that this was just pretend.

Allyson Smith has crushed on her boss for years, but never dared to make a move. When she finds herself without a date to her brother's upcoming wedding, Allyson tells her family one innocent white lie: that she's been dating her boss. Unfortunately, her boss discovers her lie, and insists on posing as her boyfriend to escort her to the wedding.

Playboy billionaire Dane Prescott always has a new heiress on his arm, but he can't get his assistant Allyson out of his head. He's fought his attraction to her, until he gets caught up in her scheme of a fake relationship.

One passionate weekend with the boss has Allyson Smith questioning everything she believes in. Falling for a wealthy playboy like Dane is against the rules, but if she's just faking it what's the harm?

SOMETIMES THE HEART needs a different kind of saving... find out if Charity Thompson will find a way of saving forever in this hospital setting Best-Selling Romance by Lexy Timms

Charity Thompson wants to save the world, one hospital at a time. Instead of finishing med school to become a doctor, she chooses a different path and raises money for hospitals – new wings, equipment, whatever they need. Except there is one hospital she would be happy to never set foot in again—her fathers. So of course, he hires her to create a gala for his sixty-fifth birthday. Charity can't say no. Now she is working in the one place she doesn't want to be. Except she's attracted to Dr. Elijah Bennet, the handsome playboy chief.

Will she ever prove to her father that's she's more than a med school dropout? Or will her attraction to Elijah keep her from repairing the one thing she desperately wants to fix?

THE ONE YOU CAN'T FORGET

Emily Rose Dougherty is a good Catholic girl from mythical Walkerville, CT. She had somehow managed to get herself into a heap trouble with the law, all because an ex-boyfriend has decided to make things difficult.

Luke "Spade" Wade owns a Motorcycle repair shop and is the Road Captain for Hades' Spawn MC. He's shocked when he reads in the paper that his old high school flame has been arrested. She's always been the one he couldn't forget.

Will destiny let them find each other again? Or what happens in the past, best left for the history books?

*** This is book 1 of the Hades' Spawn MC Series. All your questions may not be answered in the first book.*

FORTUNE RIDERS MC
BILLIONAIRE BIKER
LEXY TIMMS
Download For
FREE
Lexy
Timms

THE
DEAD OF NIGHT
SERIES
USA TODAY BESTSELLING AUTHOR
LEXY TIMMS
Abduction
Bribery
Corruption

THE
HEAT OF NIGHT
SERIES
USA TODAY BESTSELLING AUTHOR
LEXY TIMMS
Depravity
Scandal
Disgrace

Don't miss out!

Visit the website below and you can sign up to receive emails whenever Lexy Timms publishes a new book. There's no charge and no obligation.

https://books2read.com/r/B-A-NNL-DIZMB

BOOKS 2 READ

Connecting independent readers to independent writers.

Did you love *Taken By The Mob Boss*? Then you should read *Payment for Sin*[1] by Lexy Timms!

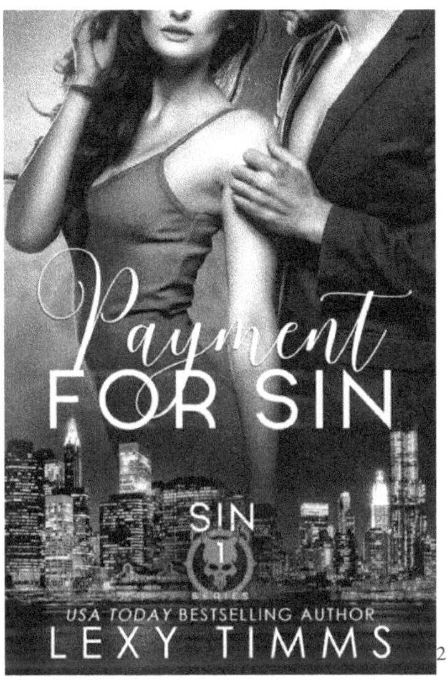

SIN will take you farther than you want to go, keep you longer than you want to stay, and cost you more than you want to pay.

Malcom "Mack O'Rourke is the son of Ian O'Rourke, one of the most notorious crime bosses in New York City. His reputation for being just as bad as his father is something he has accepted.

When his father makes a deal that confiscates the only daughter of a man who owes him a great deal of money, Mack knows it isn't going to end well for the pretty Ivy Clearwater. She's defiant and reckless and his—a gift from his father.

Mack doesn't need the complication of a woman in his life and steers clear of her until one night he can't help himself. Passion clouds

---

1. https://books2read.com/u/mKxVXV

2. https://books2read.com/u/mKxVXV

his mind and he nearly gets them both killed. When his father finds out, he threatens to get rid of Ivy.

SIN SERIES:

Book 1 – Payment for Sin

Book 2 – Atonement Within

Book 3 – Declaration of Love

Note: The author would like the reader to know that this is book 1 in a 3-book series.

Read more at www.lexytimms.com.

Also by Lexy Timms

A Bad Boy Bullied Romance
I Hate You
I Hate You A Little Bit
I Hate You A Little Bit More

A Burning Love Series
Spark of Passion
Flame of Desire
Blaze of Ecstasy

A Chance at Forever Series
Forever Perfect
Forever Desired
Forever Together

A Dark Mafia Romance Series
Taken By The Mob Boss

A Dating App Series
I've Been Matched
You've Been Matched
We've Been Matched

A "Kind of" Billionaire
Taking a Risk
Safety in Numbers
Pretend You're Mine

A Maybe Series
Maybe I Should
Maybe I Shouldn't
Maybe I Did

Assisting the Boss Series
Billion Reasons
Duke of Delegation
Late Night Meetings
Delegating Love
Suitors and Admirers

BBW Romance Series
Capturing Her Beauty

Pursuing Her Dreams
Tracing Her Curves

Beating the Biker Series
Making Her His
Making the Break
Making of Them

Betrayal at the Bay Series
Devil's Bay
Devil's Deceit

Billionaire Banker Series
Banking on Him
Price of Passion
Investing in Love
Knowing Your Worth
Treasured Forever
Banking on Christmas
Billionaire Banker Box Set Books #1-3

Billionaire CEO Brothers
Tempting the Player
Late Night Boardroom
Reviewing the Perfomance
Result of Passion

Directing the Next Move
Touching the Assets

Billionaire Holiday Romance Series
Driving Home for Christmas
The Valentine Getaway
Cruising Love
Billionaire Holiday Romance Box Set

Billionaire in Disguise Series
Facade
Illusion
Charade

Billionaire Secrets Series
The Secret
Freedom
Courage
Trust
Impulse
Billionaire Secrets Box Set Books #1-3

Blind Sight Series
See Me
Fix Me
Eyes On Me

Counting the Billions
Counting the Days
Counting On You
Counting the Kisses

Cry Wolf Reverse Harem Series
Beautiful & Wild
Misunderstood
Never Tamed

Darkest Night Series
Savage
Vicious
Brutal
Sinful
Fierce

Diamond in the Rough Anthology
Billionaire Rock
Billionaire Rock - part 2

Dirty Little Taboo Series
Flirting Touch
Denying Pleasure

Forbidding Desire
Craving Passion

Dominating PA Series
Her Personal Assistant - Part 1
Her Personal Assistant - Part 2
Her Personal Assistant Box Set

Fake Billionaire Series
Faking It
Temporary CEO
Caught in the Act
Never Tell A Lie
Fake Christmas
Fake Billionaire Box Set #1-3

Firehouse Romance Series
Caught in Flames
Burning With Desire
Craving the Heat
Firehouse Romance Complete Collection

Forging Billions Series
Dirty Money
Petty Cash
Payment Required

For His Pleasure
Elizabeth
Georgia
Madison

Fortune Riders MC Series
Billionaire Biker
Billionaire Ransom
Billionaire Misery
Fortune Riders Box Set - Books #1-3

Fragile Series
Fragile Touch
Fragile Kiss
Fragile Love

Great Temptation Series
The Devil's Footsteps
Heaven's Command
Mortals Surrender

Hades' Spawn Motorcycle Club
One You Can't Forget
One That Got Away

One That Came Back
One You Never Leave
One Christmas Night
Hades' Spawn MC Complete Series

Hard Rocked Series
Rhyme
Harmony
Lyrics

Heart of Stone Series
The Protector
The Guardian
The Warrior

Heart of the Battle Series
Celtic Viking
Celtic Rune
Celtic Mann
Heart of the Battle Series Box Set

Heistdom Series
Master Thief
Goldmine
Diamond Heist
Smile For Me

Your Move
Green With Envy
Saving Money

Highlander Wolf Series
Pack Run
Pack Land
Pack Rules

Hollyweird Fae Series
Inception of Gold
Disruption of Magic
Guardians of Twilight

How To Love A Spy
The Secret
The Secret Life
The Secret Wife

Just About Series
About Love
About Truth
About Forever
Just About Box Set Books #1-3

Justice Series
Seeking Justice
Finding Justice
Chasing Justice
Pursuing Justice
Justice - Complete Series

Karma Series
Walk Away
Make Him Pay

Kissed by Billions
Kissed by Passion
Kissed by Desire
Kissed by Love

Leaning Towards Trouble
Trouble
Discord
Tenacity

Love on the Sea Series
Ships Ahoy
Rough Sea

Billionaire in Control
Billionaire Makes Millions
Billionaire at Work
Precious Little Thing
Priceless Love
Valentine Love
The Cost of Freedom
Trick or Treat
The Night Before Christmas
Gift for the Boss - Novella 3.5
Managing the Bosses Box Set #1-3
Managing the Bosses Novellas

Mislead by the Bad Boy Series
Deceived
Provoked
Betrayed

Model Mayhem Series
Shameless
Modesty
Imperfection

Moment in Time
Highlander's Bride
Victorian Bride
Modern Day Bride
A Royal Bride

Forever the Bride

Mountain Millionaire Series
Close to the Ridge
Crossing the Bluff
Climbing the Mount

My Best Friend's Sister
Hometown Calling
A Perfect Moment
Thrown in Together

My Darker Side Series
Darkest Hour
Time to Stop
Against the Light

Neverending Dream Series
Neverending Dream - Part 1
Neverending Dream - Part 2
Neverending Dream - Part 3
Neverending Dream - Part 4
Neverending Dream - Part 5

Outside the Octagon

Submit
Fight
Knockout

Protecting Diana Series
Her Bodyguard
Her Defender
Her Champion
Her Protector
Her Forever
Protecting Diana Box Set Books #1-3

Protecting Layla Series
His Mission
His Objective
His Devotion

Racing Hearts Series
Rush
Pace
Fast

Regency Romance Series
The Duchess Scandal - Part 1
The Duchess Scandal - Part 2

Reverse Harem Series
Primals
Archaic
Unitary

RIP Series
Track the Ripper
Hunt the Ripper
Pursue the Ripper

R&S Rich and Single Series
Alex Reid
Parker
Sebastian

Saving Forever
Saving Forever - Part 1
Saving Forever - Part 2
Saving Forever - Part 3
Saving Forever - Part 4
Saving Forever - Part 5
Saving Forever - Part 6
Saving Forever Part 7
Saving Forever - Part 8
Saving Forever Boxset Books #1-3

Spanked Series
Passion
Playmate
Pleasure

Spelling Love Series
The Author
The Book Boyfriend
The Words of Love

Taboo Wedding Series
He Loves Me Not
With This Ring
Happily Ever After

Tattooist Series
Confession of a Tattooist
Surrender of a Tattooist
Heart of a Tattooist
Hopes & Dreams of a Tattooist

Tennessee Romance
Whisky Lullaby
Whisky Melody

Whisky Harmony

The Bad Boy Alpha Club
Battle Lines - Part 1
Battle Lines

The Brush Of Love Series
Every Night
Every Day
Every Time
Every Way
Every Touch
The Brush of Love Series Box Set Books #1-3

The Debt
The Debt: Part 1 - Damn Horse
The Debt: Complete Collection

The Fire Inside Series
Dare Me
Defy Me
Burn Me

The Gentleman's Club Series
Gambler

Player
Wager

The Golden Mail
Hot Off the Press
Extra! Extra!
Read All About It
Stop the Press
Breaking News
This Just In
The Golden Mail Box Set Books #1-3

The Lucky Billionaire Series
Lucky Break
Streak of Luck
Lucky in Love

The Sound of Breaking Hearts Series
Disruption
Destroy
Devoted

The University of Gatica Series
The Recruiting Trip
Faster
Higher

Stronger
Dominate
No Rush
University of Gatica - The Complete Series

T.N.T. Series
Troubled Nate Thomas - Part 1
Troubled Nate Thomas - Part 2
Troubled Nate Thomas - Part 3

Toxic Touch Series
Noxious
Lethal
Willful
Tainted
Craved

Undercover Series
Perfect For Me
Perfect For You
Perfect For Us

Unknown Identity Series
Unknown
Unpublished
Unexposed

Unsure
Unwritten
Unknown Identity Box Set: Books #1-3

Unlucky Series
Unlucky in Love
UnWanted
UnLoved Forever

War Torn Letters Series
My Sweetheart
My Darling
My Beloved

Wet & Wild Series
Stormy Love
Savage Love
Secure Love

Worth It Series
Worth Billions
Worth Every Cent
Worth More Than Money

You & Me - A Bad Boy Romance

Just Me
Touch Me
Kiss Me

Standalone
Wash
Loving Charity
Summer Lovin'
Love & College
Billionaire Heart
First Love
Frisky and Fun Romance Box Collection
Beating Hades' Bikers
Everyone Loves a Bad Boy

Watch for more at www.lexytimms.com.

About the Author

"Love should be something that lasts forever, not is lost forever." Visit USA TODAY BESTSELLING AUTHOR, LEXY TIMMS https://www.facebook.com/SavingForever *Please feel free to connect with me and share your comments. I love connecting with my readers.* Sign up for news and updates and freebies - I like spoiling my readers! http://eepurl.com/9i0vD website: www.lexytimms.com Dealing in Antique Jewelry and hanging out with her awesome hubby and three kids, Lexy Timms loves writing in her free time. MANAGING THE BOSSES is a bestselling 10-part series dipping into the lives of Alex Reid and Jamie Connors. Can a secretary really fall for her billionaire boss?

Read more at www.lexytimms.com.

9 789872 295228